AS RED
AS BLOOD

SALLA
SIMUKKA

Translated from the Finnish by **Owen F. Witesman**

HOT
KEY
BOOKS

First published in Great Britain in 2014 by Hot Key Books
Northburgh House, 10 Northburgh Street, London EC1V 0AT

Original edition published in Finnish by Tammi Publishers in 2013.
Hot Key Books edition published by agreement with Tammi Publishers and Elina
Ahlback Literary Agency, Helsinki, Finland.

Original text copyright © 2013 Salla Simukka
Translation copyright © 2014 Owen F. Witesman
With thanks to the Finnish Literature Exchange

The moral rights of the author and translator have been asserted.

A CIP catalogue record for this book is available from the British Library.
ISBN: 978-1-4714-0246-3

1

This book is typeset in 10.5 Berling LT Std using Atomik ePublisher
Printed and bound by Clays Ltd, St Ives Plc

Hot Key Books supports the Forest Stewardship Council (FSC),
the leading international forest certification organisation, and is committed to
printing only on Greenpeace-approved FSC-certified paper.
www.hotkeybooks.com

Hot Key Books is part of the Bonnier Publishing Group
www.bonnierpublishing.com

AS RED
AS BLOOD

Once upon a time in midwinter, as flakes of snow fell like feathers from heaven, a queen sat sewing at her window, which was framed in black ebony wood.

As she sewed, gazing out at the snow, the needle pricked her finger, bringing forth three drops of blood, which fell onto the snow. Seeing the beauty of the red upon the white, she thought within herself, 'Would that I had a child as white as snow, as red as blood, and as black as the wood in this window frame.'

SUNDAY, 28 FEBRUARY

1

All around lay glittering white. Over the old snow, a new, clean layer of soft flakes had fallen fifteen minutes earlier. Fifteen minutes earlier everything had still been possible. The world had looked beautiful, the future flickering somewhere in the distance, brighter, freer, more peaceful. That was worth betting everything on one last card. Trying to make a clean break was a terrible risk but the only way forward.

Fifteen minutes earlier a light, downy snowfall had spread a thin feather blanket over the old snow. Then it had ceased, as suddenly as it had begun, followed by rays of sunshine breaking through the clouds. Hardly any days all winter had been this beautiful.

Now each moment saw more red intermingling with the white, spreading, gaining ground, creeping forward through the crystals, staining them as it went. Some of the red had flown further, a shrieking bright crimson spattering the snow.

Natalia Smirnova stared with brown eyes at the red-flecked snow, seeing nothing. Thinking nothing. Hoping nothing. Fearing nothing.

Ten minutes earlier Natalia had hoped and feared more than

ever before in her life. With trembling hands she had stuffed banknotes into her genuine Louis Vuitton handbag, all the while listening for even the tiniest rustling from outside. She had tried to steady her nerves, assuring herself that everything was fine. She had a plan. But at the same time she had known that no plan was ever perfect. An intricate edifice carefully constructed over months can collapse at the barest nudge.

The handbag had also contained a passport and plane ticket to Moscow. She wasn't taking anything else. At Moscow airport, her brother would be waiting with a rental car, ready to drive her hundreds of kilometres to a *dacha* only a few people knew about. There her mother would be waiting with three-year-old Olga, the daughter she hadn't seen in more than a year. Would her little girl even remember her? But no matter. A month or two hiding out in the countryside would give them time to get to know each other again. While they waited until she believed they were safe. While they waited until the world forgot about Natalia Smirnova.

Natalia had stifled the nagging voice in her head that insisted no one would forget her at all. That they would not allow her to disappear. She had assured herself that she was not so important that they couldn't simply replace her when the need arose. And going to the effort of tracking her down would be too much bother anyway.

In this line of work, people disappeared now and then. Usually taking some money along with them. That was just one of the risks of doing business, an unavoidable loss like the spoiled fruit a supermarket had to toss out.

Natalia hadn't counted the money. She had simply stuffed as

much of it as she could in her bag. Some of the notes had got crumpled, but that didn't matter. A crumpled €500 note was worth just as much as an unwrinkled one. You could still buy three months' of food with it, maybe four if you were really careful. You could still use it to buy one person's silence for long enough. For many people, €500 was the price of a secret.

Natalia Smirnova, age twenty, lay face-down, her cheek in the cold snow. Not feeling the prickling of the ice against her skin. Not feeling the frigid chill of twenty-five degrees below on her bare earlobes.

The land is strange, and cold is its spring
Natalia, you are freezing

The man had sung that to her in a gruff voice, off-key. Natalia hadn't liked the song. The Natalia in it was from Ukraine, but she was from Russia. She had liked the man singing and stroking her hair though. She had just tried not to listen to the words. Fortunately that had been easy. She had known some Finnish, understanding much more than she could speak, but when she stopped struggling and let her mind relax, the foreign words ran together, losing their meaning and becoming nothing more than combinations of sounds falling out of the man's mouth as he hummed against Natalia's neck.

Five minutes earlier Natalia had been thinking about that man and his slightly clumsy hands. Would he miss her? Maybe a bit. Maybe just a little bit. But not enough, because he had never loved her, not really. If he had loved her, really loved her, he would have solved Natalia's problems for her, as he had promised so many times. Now Natalia had to solve her problems for herself.

Two minutes earlier Natalia had snapped shut her handbag, bulging with cash. Quickly she had tidied up and then glanced at herself in the front hall mirror. Bleached blonde hair, brown eyes, thin eyebrows, and shining red lips. She had been pale, with dark circles under her eyes from staying up too late. She had just been leaving. In her mouth she had tasted freedom and fear, both of which had a metallic tang.

Two minutes earlier she had looked her reflection in the eye and raised her chin. This was her opportunity to make a break, and she was taking it.

Natalia had heard the key turning in the lock. She had frozen in place, straining her ears. One set of footsteps, then another and a third. The Troika. The Troika were coming through the door.

All she could do was run.

One minute earlier Natalia had charged through the kitchen towards the terrace door. She had fumbled with the lock. Her hands had been shaking so much she couldn't get the door unlatched. Then, by some miracle, it had opened, and Natalia had run across the snow-covered terrace into the garden. Her leather boots had sunk into the snowdrifts, but she had pressed on without looking back. She had not heard anything. She had thought for a moment that she might make it after all, that she might escape, that she might actually win.

Thirty seconds earlier a pistol fitted with a silencer had fired with a dull snap and a bullet had pierced the back of Natalia Smirnova's coat and then her skin, barely missing her spine and ripping through her internal organs and finally the handle of her Louis Vuitton bag, which she had been clutching to her chest. She had fallen forward into the pure, untouched snow.

8

Now the red puddle under Natalia continued to spread, consuming the snow all around. The red was still voracious and warm but cooled as each second passed. One set of slow, heavy footfalls approached Natalia Smirnova lying in the snow. But she did not hear.

MONDAY, 29 FEBRUARY,
EARLY MORNING

2

Three people jostled at a door, each wanting to be first inside.

'Hey, give me a little space so I can get this key into the hole.'

'You can never get anything in the hole.'

Laughter, shushing, more laughter.

'Hold on. That's it. Got it. And now turn slowly. Very slowly. Wow. This is amazing. I mean, can you believe that you can unlock a door just by turning a key? How did anyone ever come up with a system like this? If you ask me, this is the thirteenth wonder of the world.'

'Shut up and open the door.'

Pushing the door wide, the three crowded inside. One of them almost fell. Another started making little high-pitched squeals and then laughed at how they echoed in the large, empty space. The third scratched his head and then punched in the code for the burglar alarm one digit at a time.

'One . . . seven . . . three . . . two. Hell yeah, I got it! And this is the fourteenth wonder of the world. That you can turn off an alarm by punching in some numbers. Hell yeah. Now I know what I'm gonna be when I grow up. I'm gonna be a locksmith. That's a job, right? Doing stuff with locks, I mean?

Or maybe I'll be a security guard.'

The other two weren't listening, instead running along the empty corridors in the dark, shouting and giggling. The third set off after them. Laughter ricocheted off the walls, reverberating up the stairs.

'We are the champions!'

Ampions. Mpions. Pions. Ions. Ons. Ns. S.

'And super fucking rich!'

Colliding on purpose, they fell to the floor, rolling around and snickering. Making angels on the tiled floor. Then one of them remembered.

'We're rich, but the money is dirty.'

'Yeah. Dirty money money money.'

'We were supposed to go to the darkroom. That's why we came.'

If they could just remember what had happened. Their memories were like a mist with glimpses of individual events flashing into view at random intervals. Someone vomiting. Others skinny-dipping in a pool. A locked door that shouldn't have been locked. A broken crystal vase and shards that cut someone's foot. Blood. Music throbbing too loudly. *Oops, I did it again*. A dead and buried single someone had put on repeat; who knew why. *I played with your heart, got lost in a game*. Someone crying inconsolably, sobbing that she didn't want help. The floor slick with spilled rum that smelled simultaneously sharp and sweet.

The memories refused to fit in any logical order. Who had brought the plastic bag? When had he brought it? Who had opened it, put their hand in, jerked it back out and licked their finger? When had they understood?

Have to take something. Fast. Now.

'You guys got anything left? I could use another hit.'

'I got these.'

Three pills. One for each. Together they placed them on their tongues and let them dissolve.

'That's got kick. Oh yeah. Nice kick.'

In the darkroom. Darkness. Then one of them flipped the switch.

'Let there be light. And there was light.'

Plastic bag onto the table. Bag open.

'Oh my God that stinks.'

'The money ain't the thing that stinks. Money never stinks.'

'That's a shitload of cash.'

'And we're splitting it fifty-fifty, three ways.'

'This is so sick! Nothing like this has ever happened to me. I love you guys. I love the whole world.'

'No kissing. I'll get all horny and lose my focus.'

'We could shag right here on the floor.'

'No shagging either. Now it's time to do some cleaning.'

Processing trays. Water. Cash.

Then all they had to do was hang each banknote up to dry.

'Now this is what I call money laundering.'

MONDAY, 29 FEBRUARY

3

'Up and at 'em! Come on, get up, sleepyhead. Don't even think about rolling over!'

Shouting filled Lumikki Andersson's ears. Unfortunately, the braying voice was all too familiar since it was her own. She had recorded herself on her phone as an alarm because she thought that would get her out of a warm bed better than anything else. And it worked. Rolling over didn't even cross her mind.

Sitting bleary-eyed on the edge of her bed, she glanced at the Moomin cartoon calendar hanging on the wall. Monday, 29 February. Leap day. The most pointless day in the world. Why couldn't it be an international holiday? It was just a leftover day, so why did anybody have to do anything useful or productive on it?

Lumikki shoved her feet into her blue furry slippers and trudged to her kitchen nook. Measuring out water and coffee, she put the Moka Express on the stove to percolate. She wasn't going to join the land of the living this morning without a strong cup of espresso. Outside it was still dark, far too dark to be awake. Without any light to reflect, even the tall snowdrifts didn't help. The gloom wasn't going to let up for ages yet, holding all of Finland in its suffocating grip far into March.

She hated this part of the winter. Snow and cold. Too much of both. Spring wasn't just around the corner. Winter just went on and on without giving any hope of ending, slowing the world as it froze out of sheer boredom. She was cold at home. She was cold outside. She was cold at school. Paradoxically, sometimes she felt as if the only place she wasn't cold was swimming in the hole they kept open in the ice down at the swimming beach, but she couldn't spend all her time there. Pulling on a big, grey woollen sweater, Lumikki poured herself a cup of coffee. Then she went into the only real room in her studio apartment, a princely seventeen metres square, and curled up in a beat-up armchair to try to warm up. A draught came from the window, even though she had added extra weather stripping in the autumn.

The coffee tasted like coffee. But she didn't expect anything more from it. She couldn't stand all those strange sugary chocolate hazelnut cardamom vanilla coffees. Coffee black and strong, facts straight up, and an apartment made for living in. That was how she liked to live her life.

Her mum was shocked the last time she visited. 'Don't you want to decorate at all? Make it look like a home?' No, she didn't. Lumikki had been living in her apartment for about a year and a half. Just a thick mattress on the floor as her bed, a desk, a laptop, and a comfy chair. For the first few months, her mum had insisted that she was going to buy Lumikki a bed frame and a bookcase, but Lumikki had tenaciously refused. Her books were in piles on the floor. The only 'decorative element' was the black-and-white Moomin calendar. Why would she go to the trouble of nesting? This wasn't reality TV. She was just living here while she finished high school. This studio apartment wasn't a home in the sense that she was going to put down roots for any longer than she had to. When high school was done, Lumikki would be free to go wherever she wanted without having to miss anyone or anything.

And home wasn't seventy miles south in Riihimäki with her parents either. Nowadays she felt like a stranger there. The furniture and decorations reminded her of things she preferred to forget. Thing she remembered quite often enough in her dreams and nightmares.

Her parents' reaction to her moving away from home had been full of strange contradictions. Sometimes it seemed as though it was a relief for them. It was true that the mood at home had been tense, but it had always been like that. At least as long as Lumikki could remember. She had never figured out where the tension came from, because she had never really seen Mum and Dad fighting or ever raised her own voice at them. As the move approached, her mother and father had given her frequent, long hugs, which was strange and a little irritating, since that wasn't how their family was.

After the hugs, her mother would take Lumikki's face in her hands and look at her so long that it got a little weird.

'All we have is you. Only you.'

Her mum had repeated that, looking as if she might burst into tears at any second. Lumikki had started feeling harassed. When she finally got her belongings moved to Tampere with her parents' help and closed the door for the first time after they left, she felt as if a heavy weight she didn't even know

21

she was carrying had fallen off her shoulders.

'Are you sure you're going to be okay here?'

Her mum always asked that. Her dad had a more practical approach.

'*Flickan blir snart myndig. Hon mäste ju klara sig,*' he would say, speaking Swedish to her instead of Finnish, like he always did. And that was exactly what she was going to do. Daddy's grown-up *flicka* was going to cope. A little better every day.

The girl who looked back at her from the bathroom mirror this morning was tired. The caffeine was working its way through her body too slowly. Washing her face with cold water, Lumikki pulled her brown hair back in a ponytail. Her parents had slapped her with a name that had no connection to reality. Her hair wasn't black, her skin didn't shine like freshly fallen snow and her lips weren't strikingly red. Seriously, who named their daughter after Snow White? It wasn't quite as bad in Finnish – Lumikki was an actual name, even if it was also the character in the Brothers Grimm fairy tale – but still. Why couldn't they have given her a Swedish name from Dad's side of the family? Of course she could have made the image in the mirror match her name with some hair dye and make-up, but she didn't see any point in that. Seeing her real reflection in the looking glass was enough for her, and other people's opinions were irrelevant.

Lumikki thought about what to wear to school for precisely three seconds. Then she decided to keep on her grey sweater and pulled on some jeans. Combat boots, black wool jacket, green scarf and mittens, grey skull cap. Fjällräven backpack.

Hunger gnawed at her stomach. Not even a light had greeted

her in the refrigerator. The bulb had been broken for a couple of weeks, and she hadn't felt like changing it. She would have to buy a sandwich at the school snack bar. Maybe two. And definitely more coffee.

A familiar, hectic clamour washed over her at the doors to the school. Everyone was in a hurry and needed to shout about what a hurry they were in. High-school students were so articulate, so scintillatingly creative in their modes of expression. Lumikki knew she was being mean, but some mornings tolerating the colourful clothing and dramatic gestures was tough. And then there was the unspoken agreement everyone seemed to have about the limits they would stick to so they could all be 'different' and 'unique' in more or less the same way. Underneath her irritation Lumikki was thankful though. Going to this school was a privilege. She didn't have to be in Riihimäki any more. Getting away from there had been the reason for applying here. Her parents might have had a hard time accepting a move so far away to such a big city otherwise, but landing a prestigious spot in an elite school for the arts was a good enough reason. And during her first few terms, Lumikki had felt like she had died and gone to heaven. That feeling had faded gradually though as she settled into a routine and started to see how much jealousy, affectation, pretence, self-aggrandisement and insecurity hid behind all the happy smiles.

Fortunately, the school wasn't only noisy, it was also warm, and gradually Lumikki's stiff limbs began waking up. She knew the unbearable tingling was about to start as the blood started circulating to her toes and fingers again. She should have worn

23

two pairs of wool socks and crammed them into her boots. Tossing her coat onto a hook, Lumikki ran downstairs to the lunchroom and adjoining snack bar.

'Veggies today, or just plain?' the cook asked when she saw Lumikki.

'One of each, please,' she replied. 'And a large coffee.'

'And no need to leave room for milk,' the cook said with a laugh as she filled the paper cup to the brim.

Lumikki sat down at a table and let the warmth slowly sink into her body. Ouch, ouch, ouch. There was no way around that prickling sensation. For a second she held her hands around the coffee cup and then took a bite of her sandwich. The roll was big and tasty, the tomato was ripe, and the pepper was crisp. Lumikki was a personal-budget vegetarian. She didn't buy meat with her own money. If someone else was buying and cooking it though, then she was fine eating meat. Maybe that made her a hypocrite, but it worked.

Three girls had taken over the neighbouring table. Blonde hair was swung. Dark, short hair was twirled. Red split ends were inspected. YSL Baby Doll, Britney Spears Fantasy and Miss Dior Cherie wafted through the air.

'My head's going to explode if he treats me like I'm invisible today. If he thinks he can fool around with me at parties and then ignore me at school, he needs to think again. It's hard to believe he's already eighteen.'

'My head's going to explode anyway. I shouldn't have had those last few drinks. I don't even know what was in them.'

'Well, at least we were only drinking.'

Feigned expressions of shock. Wide eyes.

24

'You don't mean . . .?'

'Well, you would've had to be blind not to notice Elisa's pupils, girl. And she was totally jittery.'

'She's always like that.'

'This was like to the hundredth power.'

Furtive glances. Three heads together, whispering. Lumikki drained her coffee cup and looked at the clock. Still ten minutes before first period. Standing, she took her plain roll and left. She couldn't stand listening to the perfume mafia at the next table, and the smell was getting unbearable.

The school social structure was relatively simple.

There were the shallow girls who mostly cared about looks and wanted to get into law or business school. They came to the arts school because they had high marks and because they were, 'you know, really creative and stuff'.

There were the great artists and even greater intellectuals for whom school was a way to show off.

There were the mathematical geniuses who always looked a little lost.

Then there were the normal, average kids who filled the corridors, jammed the stairwells, formed long lines in the cafeteria and all looked, sounded, and smelled the same. No one would remember their names in a few years. No one even remembered them now.

There were also some smart kids who were nice too though. And usually Lumikki didn't look down on the others either. She knew that the roles a lot of people played were just masks they put on at the beginning of each school day so that finding their place in the crowd would be easier. She didn't blame anyone for that. But on her very first day in high school she had decided that she wasn't going to let herself be stuffed into any category. She wasn't going to let anyone bundle her in with some reference group so people could make easy assumptions about her.

Lumikki had watched the formation of the divisions, the groupings, and the cliques with slight interest and mild amusement. She had stayed on the sidelines, on the outside. But she wasn't a loner freak sneaking along the walls dressed all in black either. People remembered her name.

Lumikki Andersson. The Swedish-Finnish girl from Riihimäki. The one who had a carefully considered opinion about everything. The one who made straight tens in physics *and* philosophy.

The one who played Ophelia so well that two teachers got mad and the rest were moved to tears.

The one who didn't participate in any of the school's pranks or parties.

The one who always ate alone but never looked lonely.

She was the puzzle piece that didn't have its own place but could suddenly fill in almost any hole you needed it to.

She wasn't like the others.

She was exactly like the others.

Lumikki approached the darkroom door and glanced down the hall to either side. No one around. Stepping into the entrance, she closed the door behind her. Darkness. Automatically, without fumbling, she opened the inner door. Her hand knew the distance from memory. Impenetrable darkness. Silence.

Peace. A moment to herself before the school day began. Zeroing out. Recharging. A daily ritual no one else knew about. A habit at once an echo of the past and an integral part of the present. For so many years Lumikki had needed to find hiding places because she was afraid. Finding secret nooks and safe havens was a lifeline. These days it wasn't so much about fear as a desire to find her own space in a place that was shared by everyone. The darkroom was a refuge where she could collect herself for a few seconds before stepping out again into the middle of all those other people's talking and sounds and opinions and feelings.

Lumikki leaned against the wall and stared into the darkness with closed eyes. Emptying her mind thought by thought. Easiest was getting rid of the day-to-day, mostly trivial concerns that revolved around the coming maths class, maybe going to the supermarket after school, maybe doing Combat in the evening. But now for some reason she couldn't even get past the surface noise. Something pushed back. Something intruded.

A smell.

The darkroom smelled different to usual. But she couldn't quite place the smell. She took a step forward. Something gently brushed against her cheek and she jumped back, turning on the red safelight.

A €500 note.

Dozens of €500 notes hanging in the darkroom to dry. Were they real? Lumikki touched the surface of the nearest one with her hand. The paper felt real at least. She looked to make sure no photographs were developing in the processing trays and then turned on the normal light.

Banknotes against the light. The watermarks were there, as were the see-through numbers. The security threads and holograms were in place. If the notes weren't genuine, they were extremely well-made forgeries.

The liquid in the processing trays was orangey-brown. Lumikki tested it with a finger. Water.

Looking at the darkroom floor, she saw it covered with reddish-brown smudges. She looked at the corner of one banknote, which had the same russet tint. Then she knew what had disturbed her in the darkness.

The stench of old, dried blood.

4

Lumikki stared out of the classroom window at the sparkling frosted trees and the old, small gravestones. But the white postcard landscape held no interest for her. Resting her eyes there was just easier than staring at the integral on the blackboard since her mind wanted to work on something besides maths.

She had left the cash in the darkroom. She had left, closed the door, and come to class. She hadn't said a word about it to anyone. One period to consider what to do.

The easiest way to get by in life was to meddle as little as possible.

That had been Lumikki's motto for years. No meddling, no messes, no sticking her nose in other people's business. If you were quiet and only spoke when you had something to say that you'd actually thought about, you got to live in peace. Even now she wanted simply to forget the whole business. Forget the banknotes washed clean of blood. Unfortunately she knew that wasn't an option. The notes were already stuck in her mind just as firmly as the smell that clung to them. She knew they wouldn't leave her in peace until she did at least something to clear up the mystery.

She should probably tell the principal. That way Lumikki

29

could pass the matter on, out of her own thoughts. Perhaps the money had something to do with some art project. But in that case, it couldn't be real. But why would someone have gone to such trouble making play money? The notes looked so real that the police would be sure to consider them forgeries, and forgery was a crime.

Or maybe the notes were real.

Lumikki couldn't think of a single good reason why someone would have decided to clean that much money in the darkroom of the high school. And what was more, then leave them there behind an unlocked door. It was ridiculous. Her brain strained to find a logical explanation but to no avail. She closed her eyes and saw the banknotes hanging from the drying lines. Some critical, decisive factor that would reveal the answer seemed to be missing from the picture in her mind. And she wasn't Sherlock Holmes, who could have taken one look and then instantly reconstructed the convoluted chain of events that led up to the cash hanging to dry in the darkroom.

Lumikki would have to speak to the principal. She should go and get the money and take it to the principal. Or should she not touch it?

The sun beat down brutally on the branches of the trees, which responded with a defiant scintillation so dazzling it was painful to the eye. Even in the warm classroom Lumikki could hear the shrieking of the cold outside. She shivered. The stagnant air in the class was mind-numbing, and her thoughts plodded forward as if wading through thick goo.

Then she made a decision.

* * *

Lumikki walked towards the darkroom, wanting to confirm what she had seen. The whole scene had been so absurd that maybe she had imagined it. Or misunderstood. What if only one of the banknotes was real and the rest was just Monopoly money?

Never jump to conclusions. That was Lumikki's second motto.

Perhaps calling them mottoes was too pompous. They were more like principles or thoughts that had proved useful or beneficial at some point.

Lumikki jumped when a boy walked around the corner. Tuukka. Eighteen years old, the son of the principal, a wannabe actor who thought he could play God's understudy if the call ever came. The teachers were amusingly adept at tolerating Tuukka's swaggering, arrogant manner of speaking and his chronic tardiness. Tuukka seemed to be in a hurry now too. He probably would have shoved Lumikki with his elbow or backpack if she hadn't discreetly dodged him.

She had learned to sidestep without people noticing her sidestepping. You had to time it properly and it had to be slight enough that it looked natural instead of caused by someone else. Lumikki had had to learn to be neither irritating nor obsequious.

Tuukka continued walking, accelerating almost to a run. He barely even noticed Lumikki. Still best to wait until he disappeared before continuing on to the darkroom though. Once she was sure he was really gone, Lumikki opened the outer door, closed it, opened the darkroom door, and turned on the red light.

Then she blinked two times.

The scene remained the same. The money was gone.

Lumikki cursed silently. This was what she got for not acting immediately. What was she going to do now? Say that she had seen thousands of euros hanging in the darkroom but had no way to prove it? Wait until someone asked her about it and then tell what she had seen? Forget the whole thing and chalk it up to a hallucination brought on by too little sleep and too much caffeine?

She leaned on the darkroom wall and closed her eyes. Something was bothering her again. Something out of place, something strange. Her brain had recorded something and now was trying to figure out what didn't belong. Lumikki opened her eyes and realized what it was.

The backpack.

Tuukka never used a backpack. He had a black leather Marimekko shoulder bag that could barely fit the books he needed on any given day. And if they didn't fit, he left some of them at home. Colourful fabric Marimekko bags were part of the standard uniform for high-school girls, but Lumikki had never seen anyone with a leather one except Tuukka. As an accessory, it landed perfectly in the grey zone between conformity and individuality, a carefully considered movement in step with the herd but with a subtle twist thrown in. But slung over one of his shoulders Tuukka now had a dingy grey backpack, frayed at the seams and stained at the corners. Definitely not in keeping with the image of a demigod descended from on high to grace mere mortals with his presence. And it had been stuffed full without looking heavy.

Lumikki could solve this equation instantly.

* * *

32

The usual morning crowd was gathered at the Central Square Coffee House: mothers with their babies and mush and conversations about sleep schedules, college girls drinking lattes that gnawed gaping holes in their monthly budgets and pretending to study for exams while really concentrating on daydreaming about the future, and a couple of men in suits with laptops playing Angry Birds or checking Facebook instead of working on PowerPoints. Coffee machines whirring and gurgling. The scent of cappuccino and hazelnuts hanging in the air. Pastries looking more delicious than they really were. The sweat that appeared instantly when you walked through the door in a winter coat.

Lumikki sat at a corner table with her back to the rest of the café as she flipped through a magazine and drank her tea. At a nearby table sat Tuukka, Elisa and Kasper.

Once Lumikki had realized that the cash was in Tuukka's backpack, she rushed after him immediately. She had snatched her coat, mittens, scarf and hat from the rack. Running out of school, she slipped and slid past the smoking spot and came to the churchyard, where she stopped and scanned for Tuukka. At the end of the park path, almost at Häme Street, she spotted the grey backpack swinging from his shoulder. Heedless of the cold air tearing at her lungs, Lumikki continued running, eventually slowing to a light jog and then a brisk walk to keep an appropriate distance. See but don't be seen. Maintain line of sight.

Her breathing, more a panting, went straight from vapour to icy glitter that stuck to her eyelashes and the locks of hair protruding from under her cap. In temperatures this far below zero, everyone appeared prematurely grey.

Lumikki had seen Tuukka enter the Coffee House and waited a few minutes before following. By then, he had already been deep in discussion with Elisa and Kasper.

Now Lumikki was doing her best to remain invisible. Inconspicuous. Fortunately she knew how to be someone else. Immediately upon entering the café, Lumikki had gone to the restroom, removed her outerwear and sweater, taken down her hair, and braided it in a side plait she never actually wore. Instead of coffee, she ordered tea. She was browsing a women's magazine, although normally she would have grabbed the sports pages or *Image*. She sat in a different way, held her hands in a different position, tilted her head like someone else.

People thought they recognised each other from a distance based on clothing or hair. Superficially that may have been true, but in reality recognising another person was a much more complicated process influenced by hundreds, perhaps thousands of different factors. Height, posture, gait, bearing, proportions of body and face, expressions, and even microexpressions that flitted by so quickly that they almost never registered consciously. That was why disguising yourself as someone else was so difficult. According to some, it was impossible without significant plastic surgery and years of practice.

But surprising small changes could trim away your most recognisable characteristics if you knew what to do. If someone had been consciously looking for Lumikki, known that she was in the coffee shop, of course they would have recognized her. But if you just scanned the room expecting a crowd of strangers, Lumikki was just another slightly hippy-looking poet girl sitting with her camomile tea. A girl with nothing conspicuously familiar about her.

So Tuukka, Elisa and Kasper took no notice of Lumikki, despite sitting almost right next to her. And besides, they had more important concerns. They had a problem.

'What are we going to do with it?' Elisa asked the boys.

As soon as she entered the coffee shop, Lumikki had noticed how terrible Elisa looked. Her skin was normally fair, but now it appeared almost grey. She had dark rings under her eyes and had been careless when she washed or wiped off her last layer of make-up. Her bleach-blonde hair clung unwashed to her head. Instead of forming a stylish ensemble, her clothing looked as if she had thrown on whatever her hand happened to land on first. Elisa never would have been caught dead looking this way at school. That she had the nerve to come to the coffee shop in such a state was a wonder.

Elisa was one of the most beautiful girls in school. She also acted the part, and her poise made others believe in her beauty even more strongly. Seeing her this way, exhausted and scared, you realised the beauty was a carefully constructed mask whose single most important factor was not the right colour of lip gloss or professionally applied eye shadow, but a large dose of self-confidence and flirtatiousness. Elisa's smile made boys' hearts flutter and palms sweat.

To this day Lumikki had never figured out the true nature of Elisa and Tuukka's relationship. Obviously they had dated at some point, but now they seemed to be just friends. Maybe friends with benefits. Elisa toyed with the small male population of the arts high school as she saw fit, and of course as a being descended from a higher sphere Tuukka was most girls' fantasy, but some other glue seemed to bind them together too. Maybe they imagined that as the alphas of the school they were so far above everyone else that they could never consider a serious dating relationship with anyone else.

'What should we do? Duh. We should keep it, of course. And keep our mouths shut,' Kasper said.

Lumikki wondered how Kasper had earned his place at the school. He seemed to concentrate more on ditching class than doing homework. The whispers in the hall said he was on the verge of expulsion if things didn't change. Kasper dressed in black and wore flamboyant gold jewellery. Keeping his hair slicked back required a significant amount of gel, and in his world he clearly thought he was some sort of bling-bling rap artist even though in reality his performances evoked more pity than excitement in the audience. Kasper was an odd fish, and you couldn't tell whether he was a chump or an actual small-time thug. For ages Lumikki had wondered why Elisa and Tuukka hung out with Kasper at all. Elisa glanced around and lowered her voice.

'We can't keep it,' she said. The panic in her voice was audible.

'What do you think we should do then?' Tuukka asked. 'Go tell the police?'

Kasper snickered. Elisa's dad was a cop. Occasionally she received good-natured and sometimes less good-natured ribbing about that fact.

'It isn't ours. We ended up with it by accident. Someone out there is looking for it, and if they find us, we're screwed.'

Elisa was desperate to convince the boys.

'Come on, use your head. What can we really do? How can we explain everything that happened without getting caught ourselves? We should have done something right then that night,' Tuukka pointed out.

'We did do something,' Kasper said, chortling.

Elisa sighed. 'Yeah. We acted like regular geniuses.'

'It seemed logical at the time,' Tuukka said. 'But you get what I'm saying. If we tell about the . . . it . . . we have to tell about everything else. And I don't know about you, but I can't afford that.'

'Neither can I,' Kasper said.

Lumikki listened as Elisa's fingernails drummed nervously on the tabletop.

'My memory might be a little too fuzzy to say anything for sure. I can't sort out what happened when. Mostly I just know that our house was a godawful mess in the morning. You don't even want to hear all the places I found puke.'

'You've probably got a lot of scrubbing to do so your dad doesn't catch on that you weren't just sitting at home studying physics all weekend.' Kasper leaned back on his chair with an amused expression on his face.

'Are you crazy? Today's when the cleaner comes. She's working on it right now. I promised to pay her double if she does it in half the usual time and keeps her mouth shut. If I could just remember everything then maybe I could . . .'

'Get us all in really, really big trouble? That sounds like an awesome plan.' Tuukka's voice had a hard, threatening tone.

Elisa was silent for a moment. At the next table, someone

made it to the next level on Angry Birds and gave a satisfied 'Yes!'

'Okay,' Elisa said. 'So we'll keep our mouths shut. For now. We wait and see what happens. But I have to say I have a really bad feeling about this.'

'Maybe ten grand will warm you up,' Tuukka said.

'What? No, I don't want any.'

'Of course you do. I've got three bags. Ten thousand each. We're all in this together.'

There was a rustling and the sound of a zipper as Tuukka opened the backpack under the table. Lumikki turned her head slightly and watched out of the corner of her eye as two black plastic bags were transferred under the table from Tuukka's backpack to Elisa and Kasper's bags.

Elisa pressed her face in her hands and gave an anguished sigh. 'Fuck. This morning when I woke up I was so hoping this was all just a bad dream.'

'No one saw you, did they?' Kasper asked Tuukka.

'No.'

'And no one had been in the darkroom?' Kasper asked.

'And left all that just hanging there? I seriously doubt it.'

But there was tension in Tuukka's laugh. Suddenly he stood up.

'This meeting is done. You can leave now.'

'I'm still drinking my chai,' Elisa said.

'If I was you, I wouldn't hang around town looking like that any longer than I had to,' Tuukka said. 'And I mean that with all the love in the world, baby.'

'Yeah. You're one to talk,' Elisa threw back, but she got up.

Lumikki waited until the trio had left. Then she tried to gulp down the rest of her tea. What the hell? Did people really drink this stuff voluntarily? She ended up leaving the dregs of the over-priced dishwater in her cup. When a safe amount of time had passed, she bundled up and stepped back out into the biting cold. On the way home she would have time to think.

5

A bitter, electric-cold wind was blowing on the stone bridge over the rapids that ran through the middle of the city. Lumikki hurried her steps, analysing what she had heard. Tuukka, Elisa and Kasper had ended up with the money somehow the night before. How, Lumikki didn't know. Whose was the money? Did they even know? Maybe not. Probably not. They seemed even more lost than usual about what had happened the previous night.

The money had obviously been bloody already, and the three of them had come up with the genius idea of washing it in the school darkroom. That was the hardest thing to understand. Who would ever think to go to the school in the middle of the night to clean a pile of dirty money?

At least we were only drinking.

Suddenly the words of the perfume mafia started echoing in Lumikki's head. So people must have been taking something else at the party last night. Some of them at least. Maybe Elisa, Tuukka and Kasper. That would explain why they had come up with such a crazy solution. And that would explain why they couldn't say exactly what happened.

A policeman's daughter. A principal's son. The scenario was so classic it made Lumikki shudder. Kids from good families desperate to be rebellious? Dangerous games because they couldn't get enough kicks from anything else? Or did they just want to get really messed up?

People were sliding all over the place by the traffic lights at the intersection by the train station. No amount of gravel the city spread around was enough to ensure traction in a place where thousands of pairs of feet polished the ice every day. Lumikki let her combat boots slap harder on the ground.

The situation had become significantly more complicated. She didn't want to go talk to the principal. Or the police. She didn't want to get involved at all, even though the trio weren't her friends in any way. They didn't mean anything to her. But she also didn't want to end up in the centre of the whirlwind that would undoubtedly blow up if she snitched.

An anonymous tip to the police? That was definitely one option. Would they take it seriously? Probably, if someone had reported €30,000 missing. And if they didn't take her seriously, it wouldn't be her problem any more. She would have done her duty.

As she approached Tammela, Lumikki felt a strange surge of emotion. Her apartment was not her home, that was clear, but had she started to soften to the neighbourhood? That thought amused her. Black sausage and milk at Tammela Square. The shouts of TPV supporters from the Tammela Football Stadium. Basic stuff all the locals did. Nostalgia for the few wooden buildings left from old Tammela and veneration for the red-brick buildings of the former Aaltonen Shoe Factory.

That didn't sound at all like Lumikki Andersson, who avoided all superfluous pathos. But for some reason she felt a little more relaxed and a little warmer here than in other parts of town. Neighbourhood pride weren't words that existed in her vocabulary, but there were probably worse things in the world than liking where you lived. Perhaps this neighbourhood could become her home. Perhaps she could start thinking of these streets as her own. Perhaps that had already happened, even though consciously Lumikki didn't want to get too attached to any one place.

The shouts and laughter and cries of children echoed from the yard of the Tammela School. Lumikki watched as the girls and boys ran and jumped and swung and climbed, their breath steaming and their cheeks red from the cold. In their thick winter clothing they were like pudgy, colourful snowmen. Her gaze scanned the edges of the schoolyard for the lonely children abandoned by their peers. She focused her ears to pick out the cries of genuine fear from the shouts of joy. Lumikki knew that for some this schoolyard glittering in the winter sun was a nightmare kingdom where the days were long and as black as night.

A little girl walked around the lemon-coloured Art Nouveau school building by herself. She walked slowly, head held down. Lumikki watched the girl for a moment. Did she turn at each corner to glance behind her? Did she flinch every now and then? Was that anguish residing in her downcast eyes? No. When Lumikki could finally make out the girl's face, she found her smiling to herself. The girl's lips were moving. She was probably creating a story in her mind that made her eyes smile along too.

42

That girl isn't like I was then, Lumikki thought. Fortunately not.

Then she realised that something was amiss. Something was wrong. Someone was too close.

She realised too late.

Suddenly strong hands grabbed her and dragged her into the shadows of a nearby doorway, shoving her violently against the stone wall. Lumikki's cheek pressed hard against the frigid rock. The surprise attack left Lumikki's arms limp as her assailant pulled them painfully behind back her. Lumikki barely managing to contain a yelp.

She recognised her attacker from his smell before he said a single word.

Tuukka.

'You're not the only one who knows how to tail someone.'

Tuukka's words came with an unpleasant warmth on her cheek. His breath stank of the coffee he had just drunk and a recently smoked cigarette. Lumikki could have slapped herself. How could she have made such an elementary mistake? How could she have left the coffee shop without watching her back?

Never overestimate your own cleverness. Never think you are completely safe. She should have learned by now. Her skills had grown rusty in Tampere since she didn't need them every day any more.

'I noticed you in the coffee shop. Well, not you, just this backpack of yours. And then I realised that I almost ran into you back near the darkroom. Quite a coincidence, isn't it,' Tuukka said, squeezing Lumikki's arm.

Lumikki did a quick evaluation of the situation.

43

If she moved fast enough, she might be able to wrench free of Tuukka's grasp. That wasn't guaranteed though. And Tuukka was fast. He would just catch her again. Better not to struggle and waste her strength for no reason. She might as well hear what he had to say.

'What did you see? What do you know?' Tuukka asked.

'I saw it in the darkroom earlier. And I heard what you were saying in the café. That's all,' Lumikki replied calmly.

Provoking him now wasn't going to get her anything.

'Damn it,' Tuukka said. 'Nobody can know about this.'

Lumikki did not reply. The rough, icy stone of the wall chafed her cheek. She tried to move as little as possible.

'You're going to keep your mouth shut. You aren't going to tell anyone. You don't know anything. No one would even believe you.'

Tuukka tried to sound menacing, but there was uncertainty in his voice. Lumikki still didn't speak.

'Do you hear me?'

Tuukka's voice was louder and even more uncertain. He was afraid. He was much more afraid than Lumikki.

'I hear you,' Lumikki said.

Tuukka thought for a second.

'Okay. How much do you want?' he asked.

Now his voice was almost pleading. He was clearly terrified for his reputation.

'I don't want any of it,' Lumikki replied. 'But now you're going to let me go.'

It wasn't a request or a command, simply a statement. A fact. Never give people options, just give them simple directives.

Don't beg or demand, just tell how things are. Lumikki's certainty made Tuukka release his grip, and she turned, slowly massaging her wrists.

'Now this is what we're going to do,' she said, looking the boy firmly in the eye. 'I don't have any desire to get involved in this. I haven't seen anything, and I haven't heard anything. I'm not going to rat on anyone, but if someone asks me directly I'm also not going to lie. I think you're going to get into trouble over this, and I don't have any intention of saving you.'

Tuukka looked at her hesitantly. His ears were red from the cold. He wasn't wearing a hat. Vanity seemed to trump practicality. He was clearly weighing up Lumikki's words, calculating the risks of each of his options.

'Okay. It's a deal,' he said finally, extending his hand.

Lumikki didn't take it. Tuukka ran it through his hair and laughed.

'You're a surprisingly tough chick. Maybe I've underestimated you.'

Lots of people do that, Lumikki thought.

Trying to regain the upper hand, Tuukka presumptuously brushed Lumikki's hair out of her face.

'Do you know what? You could actually be pretty good looking if you changed this horrible hairdo, ditched those Greenpeace clothes and learned to put on make-up,' he said, one corner of his mouth curling.

Lumikki smiled.

'And do you know what?' she replied. 'You could actually be a pretty smart, nice guy if you completely changed your horrible personality.'

She didn't hang around to hear what Tuukka might have to say to that and walked away, not looking back. She knew he wouldn't follow her.

At her apartment, Lumikki looked in the mirror at her red, tingling cheek. The mark was going to be visible for at least a day. It was small, and she had experienced much worse. Drinking some cold water straight from the tap, she decided not to go to school the next day. She could afford to stay home this one time. Then everything would go on as normal again. She would go to school. She would forget the money. She wouldn't get involved in any way.

TUESDAY, 1 MARCH

6

It was 3:45 a.m.

Boris Sokolov was staring at his phone like it was an oversized cockroach, wanting to smash it against the wall. The ring had woken him in the middle of a dream. He had been lied to. He had been threatened. He could tolerate being woken up. The lying disgusted him. But what Boris Sokolov truly hated was being threatened. Especially when it came from a man who shouldn't have been in any position to make threats.

Boris Sokolov switched his phone's SIM card and dialled a number.

After three beeps, the Estonian answered. His voice said that the call had woken him too. His speech seemed viscous and distant, even though he only lived a few kilometres away.

'Well?'

Boris began speaking to the Estonian in Russian. 'He called. He says the money didn't come.'

'He's crazy,' the Estonian said. 'We took it right to his house.'

Boris stood and walked to the bedroom window. The parquet floor felt cold. Maybe he should have had carpet installed. Who cared if it got dirty? He could just have it replaced every couple of years. The moonlight was unpleasantly bright. Two sets of rabbit tracks crossed in the garden. The Estonian had helped him remove another kind of tracks, tramping a natural-looking walkway to the other side of the backyard. Carefully removing any snow that was not perfectly white.

'He said he stayed up all night. Tonight.'

'What the hell? We told him it was coming at the usual time but a different place.'

The Estonian was really starting to wake up now.

Boris grunted. 'He said something about a misunderstanding. That yesterday was leap day and the last day of the month.'

He tapped his fingers on the windowsill. Had the rabbits been gnawing at the apple tree? He would have to string up some sort of fencing around the base of the trunk. Or keep watch one night and get a couple of rabbit roasts for the freezer. His own freezer, this time.

'Yeah, yeah, but the twenty-eighth doesn't turn into the twenty-ninth because of the leap year. And why was he up tonight when we already delivered the money yesterday?'

'That's just it. He says we didn't. That he hasn't seen anything. Nada.'

The Estonian was silent for a moment. Boris waited to see whether his underling would come to the same conclusion he had.

'He's bullshitting us. He did get the money. He realised what happened to it, and now he's trying to play hardball.'

Yep, same conclusion.

'The little shit tried to threaten me. He said he'd expose everything.' Boris felt himself getting angry again just saying the words. He squeezed the cell phone, imagining the exoskeleton

50

of the cockroach crunching in his fist. 'But I'll burn in hell before I see that!'

The Estonian was furious too. Good. They were firmly on the same side. Two backsliders within the past thirty-eight hours was enough. No, it was too much. Two too many. A working machine could only lose so many parts at one time without repairs.

'We're going to make sure he doesn't talk.' Boris said the words with relish. No one threatened him without repercussions. No one bullshitted him and got away with it.

He had thought a plastic bag full of blood-stained cash would have been sufficient warning.

Apparently not.

But they knew how to play hardball too. The difference was that they would win.

Terho Väisänen knew he wasn't going to be able to fall back asleep. He lay on one side of the queen-sized bed, even though he could have stretched out across the whole mattress if he wanted to. He felt as if someone were whittling the bed frame out from under him and that at any moment he might collapse onto the floor, which would also give way. Something was crumbling, something he had thought would last.

Terho Väisänen couldn't say he was proud of himself. There were mornings when he had a hard time looking himself in the eye, but usually the feeling went away by the time he reached work and remembered how much good he had done over the past ten years. How many cases had been solved solely thanks to him? That had its price, but so be it.

Pulling the covers up tight around his neck, he sniffed the fresh scent of the duvet cover. He wished he could hug someone, hold someone warm tight in his arms.

Terho tried to call one more time. The phone rang and rang, but no one answered. Terho felt a vague fear taking root somewhere around his solar plexus. He sensed that after tonight everything would be different.

7

Once upon a time there was a night that never ended. With its darkness it devoured the sun, strangling all light away and spreading its cold, black hands over the earth. The night glued the eyes of humanity shut eternally, making dreams deeper and stranger, making man and woman alike forget themselves and glide along arm in arm with imagined creatures, losing their own memories. On the walls of the buildings, the night painted its most terrifying pictures, from which all colour had fled. On the faces of the sleeping populace, the night breathed cold, suffocating air, which invaded the lungs, turning them black inside.

Gasping for air, Lumikki opened her eyes. She was covered in sweat, and the weight of her quilt felt as though it were choking her throat. She had to throw it off and sit up. Feet into slippers. To the window to look out across the park, a familiar scene that could soften the rock-hard anxiety of the nightmare to a simple uneasy hollow feeling. The moon illuminated the snowbanks, the swings and jungle gym in the playground, and the roofs of the buildings, wrapping them in a silver-foil skin. The shadows stood in place like figures painted black on the snow.

Light shone from the windows of two different apartments. Someone else was awake this morning at 3:45 a.m. A perverse time to be awake, against human nature. Only the nightmare images of dreams were abroad at this hour, indistinguishable to the human eye from the other shadows. The bottom edge of the window was decorated in a lace of frost flowers. Instinctively Lumikki touched the cold glass, even though she knew the ice crystals were on the other side. The warmth of her hand wouldn't melt them. Cold air breathed on her fingers through a chink in the window frame. Lumikki pulled her hand back and shivered.

There had been a time when she would wake up hoping the night would never end and the morning would never come. Back then she dreamed of endless nights as well, but those had been hopeful dreams. Now they were nightmares. Many things had changed. Back then Lumikki woke up in the morning disappointed that she would have to get up and face another day that was unlikely to bring anything good. She knew there would be more evil on offer than a normal person could endure. But she endured – she endured for years on end. Perhaps she was as abnormal as they had claimed.

Now Lumikki returned to her covers and warm bed. Exhaustion pressed her eyelids shut, and she didn't have any more bad dreams all night. She didn't dream any dreams at all; at least not that she remembered the next day.

Lumikki awoke again to the sun shining. It was already after ten. Her whole body felt oddly rested and refreshed. This must have been how people were supposed to feel in the morning, not like a zombie woken from the dead for the umpteenth time. She didn't think much of skipping school, but this time it had probably been a good idea. She didn't want to see Tuukka's self-satisfied face again this soon.

Lumikki stretched her legs and arms out on the bed. What would she do today? Maybe go to the gym. Her aunt Kaisa had bought her a year membership at a fitness centre for Christmas. Lumikki didn't always exactly feel at home surrounded by all the perky aerobics girls, but sweating always did her good, and she needed more strength. Tuukka had succeeded in surprising her and momentarily getting the upper hand. But if Lumikki could have trusted in her physical strength, breaking away and giving him a taste of his own cheek smashed against the cold rock wall would have been easy.

Do not seek power for revenge. Seek power in order to avoid situations that would make you want revenge. That sounded noble. In reality all it meant was that Lumikki never wanted to be at a disadvantage ever again.

She didn't want to think about the previous day. She just wanted to think about this day. Her day.

Her mum and her aunt chattered sometimes about how important it was for women to take time to pamper themselves. Pampering being a synonym for shopping, chocolate, bubble baths, women's magazines and nail polish. Lumikki shuddered. For her a day like that wouldn't be pampering, it would be an awkward charade.

For her a day of pampering meant comic books, black liquorice, serious exercise, veggie curry and, above all, solitude. Her mum always wondered how she could get along so well alone. Didn't she ever get bored? Lumikki didn't bother saying that she was more likely to get bored being around other people, listening to their pointless small talk. Better alone than in bad company. When she was alone, she could be completely herself. Free. No one demanding anything. No one talking when she wanted silence. No one touching her when she didn't want to be touched.

Lumikki also enjoyed seeing art shows. She would reserve several hours, load her phone with enough music, preferably Massive Attack, and go without any preconceptions, avoiding too much advance study of the artist or the exhibition theme. After paying the admission fee, she would enter the first gallery staring at the floor, turn on her music in her headphones, and close her eyes. She would empty her thoughts, filling her head with music. She would concentrate on breathing evenly and allow her heart rate to drop almost to resting. Once she had made the surrounding mundane world disappear, she would open her eyes and fall into the first piece.

Sometimes she completely lost her sense of time. Pictures, colours, moods, the feel of movement on the canvas or paper or photograph, the sense of depth, the irregularity and texture of the surface would drag her deep into a world she neither completely recognised nor understood, but which was still hers. Other Finns had their lakes and forests, but this was the landscape of her soul. Art spoke to her in a language that intermingled with music, forming pathways that lead to darkness or light. The subjects were rarely important to her. What the pictures depicted or whether they depicted anything at all mattered even less. All that mattered was the feeling.

Lumikki rarely departed an exhibit without getting something from it. Sometimes that did happen, but usually the reason was some external factor, like hunger or fatigue or stress. Or other people being disruptive and making so much noise that her music couldn't completely drown them out. Some shows were like tornadoes; she left gasping for air and trying to regain her balance. Some she felt like a heat in her chest for days afterwards. Some reverberated in her head. The colours persisted on her retinas, painting new shades on her dreams. She would not be the same person after a show as she was before.

Today wasn't going to be an art exhibition day though, because Lumikki had already been to see the travelling exhibitions at the Tampere Museum of Art, the Sara Hildén Art Museum and the TR1 Kunsthalle, and their permanent collections were old news too. She usually tried to attend early on in a show, but not during the very first weeks. After the art groupies were out of the way and the Johnny-come-latelies were still at home on the couch.

The sun made the frost flowers on the window glitter. Lumikki considered whether she would go for a short jog before breakfast after all. She looked at the thermometer, which read around twenty-five degrees below zero. No thanks. Breathing hard would be too much for her lungs.

Suddenly her phone rang. Lumikki picked it up. She didn't recognise the number.

Don't answer unfamiliar numbers. Not ever. That had been her motto before but not any more. These days she had to have the courage to answer those calls too, since she lived alone and handled all her own affairs.

'Lumikki Andersson,' she said in a formal tone.

'Hi, it's Elisa.'

Elisa? Why would Elisa be calling her?

'Tuukka told me that you know,' the girl continued quickly.

Lumikki sighed. She wasn't going to have to reassure Elisa too that she wasn't going to tell anyone, was she?

'I didn't know who else to call. The boys don't want to talk about it. I'm totally losing it. You have to come here. I can't stand being alone. I'm afraid. Help me.'

Elisa's voice was high-pitched, frantic. She was clearly panicked.

'Well, I don't know . . .' Lumikki began, but she didn't get any further before Elisa broke down in sobs.

Lumikki stared at the frost flowers. What if she just pressed that red button? And then switched off the phone? *Don't get involved. Don't interfere. Only worry about your own business.* Why was sticking to her mottoes so difficult now? Maybe because Elisa was crying. Maybe because no one had ever asked for her help so directly before.

'Okay, I'll come over,' she heard herself say into the phone. So much for a day to herself.

Elisa lived in Pyynikki, across the river at the base of a large, oblong hill that looked out over the city of Tampere and its surrounding lakes. The most expensive neighbourhood in the city. Lumikki felt completely out of place standing at the front gate in her shabby winter coat. A stone wall bordered the large front garden on the street side. At the back of the property began the slope of the hill, which was famous for its forested walking paths. White and stately, the house itself was shockingly large. Lumikki had always imagined at least two families living in each of these buildings, but apparently that wasn't the case, at least not here. Although, there weren't any names visible anywhere. The residents of these homes didn't want their letterboxes or door plates giving away too much about their families.

One more check of the text message. Yes, the address was correct.

Two bronze lions sat atop the stone gateposts. Each held its paws protectively on a metal ball. *Beware of lions.*

Lumikki pressed the buzzer. Within seconds, Elisa opened the front door and rushed down to the gate in a sort of pink romper outfit. Lumikki might be wearing old, threadbare clothes from a thrift shop, but at least she didn't look like an escapee from a mental hospital. Elisa opened the gate and threw her arms around Lumikki before she could dodge out of the way.

'Thank you so much for coming! I wasn't sure how you'd react since we don't know each other that well,' Elisa blubbered.

She smelled of roses and affluence. Lumikki didn't wear perfume herself, but she had trained her nose to tell them apart. She had actually become pretty good at it. There had been a time when identifying a person at a distance simply based on their perfume had given her the decisive few extra seconds she needed to escape.

'Joy by Jean Patou,' she said as she quickly extricated herself from the hug. For her, the recent cultural innovation in Finland of hugging strangers was like a stubborn cold requiring a speedy remedy.

Elisa looked at Lumikki in astonishment.

'I didn't know you were into perfume. I got this one last Christmas from my dad. They say it's the world's most expensive scent.'

'Yeah.'

Lumikki had absolutely no desire to get tangled up in some pointless conversation about perfume and Christmas presents. No small talk. She had come because Elisa had been in a panic and crying. If she was just here to be some sort of lap dog, she could turn around and go back home right now. She could still make it to Combat class.

Elisa was bouncing around like an overstimulated pink bunny. She didn't seem to have realised until now how intense the grip was of the temperature outside.

'Let's go inside,' she said.

Lumikki nodded.

Inside, the house was even more beautiful than outside. High ceilings, bay windows, blond wood, furniture that clearly cost more than Lumikki paid in rent in a year, lots of winter sunshine spilling over the floors and other surfaces without revealing a single particle of dust. The cleaner Elisa had mentioned in the coffee shop the day before had done excellent work for her double pay.

'Downstairs is the sauna and pool area,' Elisa saw fit to report as Lumikki was removing her black boots and coat and tossing her mittens, scarf and hat on the shelf above the coat hooks.

'I didn't come here to swim,' she replied curtly.

Elisa was abashed.

'Of course not. Sorry. Do you want anything? Cappuccino, mochaccino, latte?'

'Just regular coffee. Black.'

'Okay. I'll get it. You can go up and wait in my room.'

Lumikki started walking up the stairs. On the landing was a mirror where she glanced at this out-of-place girl. What the crap was she doing here? Coming had been a mistake. Despite herself she was getting sucked deeper and deeper into a swamp that was smelling worse by the minute.

Elisa's room looked like something pink and black had exploded in it. Those two colours dominated everything from the rugs to the walls and from the curtains to the laptop. Was this some sort of extended princess phase with a little punk rock sprinkled on top for street cred? The room was twice as large as Lumikki's studio apartment. There was also a door out to a small balcony.

Elisa seemed to have an endless array of jewellery and make-up. The bookshelf was full of horror movies and romantic comedies.

Lumikki looked for a flaw in the room. Every person's room had a flaw, something that didn't fit the picture, that contradicted the preconceptions.

There were two flaws in Elisa's room.

On the lowest shelf of the bookcase was a row of books on astronomy. They had been shoved down there as if to keep them out of sight, but there were enough of them that they couldn't just be the residue of a single failed gift or there by chance. And now Lumikki remembered that Elisa had always done pretty well in maths and physics.

The second flaw was a plump ball of yarn and knitting needles with the beginnings of a sweater or something on them. So Elisa didn't want everything shop bought.

Interesting. Or it would have been had Lumikki felt any desire to get to know Elisa. Now she simply registered these irregularities and tucked them away in her mind.

'Coffee, black!' Elisa announced at the door and handed Lumikki a mug.

It was black. Elisa's own cup was pink. This observation amused Lumikki momentarily. But the sociological field work could end right there.

'Why did you ask me to come here?' she asked.

Elisa sat down on her bed and sighed.

'I'm so afraid, and I don't know what I should do.'

'What do you remember about the night of the party?'

'Not much. Or, I mean, I remember a lot, but I have a hard time connecting anything.'

'Tell me from the very beginning, in as much detail as possible, what you remember about what happened at the party and how you ended up with the money,' Lumikki suggested. 'Then we can think about what would be the best course of action.'

She hated the didactic tone in her voice, but right now she had to talk to Elisa like a child. The girl's hands were shaking, even though she was squeezing her cup tightly to try to make them stop.

Slowly Elisa began telling her story, which was almost incoherent it was so full of digressions. After learning that her parents would be away from home on Sunday, she decided to throw a party. Her mother was leaving on Saturday for a week-long business trip, and her father would be gone overnight, also for work. Elisa droned on for a while about all the thought she put into who to invite and what they would drink and

62

what they would eat. *Get to the point*, Lumikki thought. This wasn't exactly what she meant by detail. If she wanted to gossip, Elisa could find another listener.

'I wanted a little more sparkle at my party. So I asked Kasper to get some pills for me and Tuukka. We've dropped them together before sometimes. You get a way better buzz than from alcohol. Too many drinks always make me want to puke.'

Elisa's sullen expression amused Lumikki. Who didn't have to puke after drinking too much? Wasn't that kind of one of the basic features of alcohol?

'Where did Kasper score them?' she asked.

'I don't know. And I don't want to. Sometimes he runs with a dodgy crowd that's best to avoid.'

A sudden virtuous tone. Elisa seemed to be remembering that she was the daughter of a police officer.

'Did anyone else take them?'

'Not that I know of. Kasper is pretty careful about who he deals to. He doesn't want to get caught.'

Of course not. Lumikki could have told her that at least the perfume mafia seemed to know perfectly well that people had been partying with more than alcohol.

'Most people started going home sometime after midnight.' Elisa laughed. 'Good little kiddies don't want to be too hung over at school the next day.'

Lumikki didn't join in the laughter, and Elisa turned serious too.

'Okay, now that I look back on it, that might have been a good move for me too. Everybody else was getting pretty drunk by that point. I know I was messed up, and that's when my

63

memory gets fuzzy. Some people were puking in the corners. Someone broke a crystal vase and got cut on the glass. The whole house was a wreck. I think I asked Tuukka to throw a couple of drunk idiots out.'

Elisa had lowered her coffee cup to her desk. She started picking at her cuticles. Her bright pink nail polish was worn off at the tips. Her hands still trembled slightly. Lumikki didn't say anything. Better to let Elisa tell her story without any leading questions. Memories were more reliable without someone else prompting them.

'By two everyone else had left except Tuukka and Kasper. We were mostly up here in my room hanging out and messing around. We didn't have to pretend any more that we were just drinking. Then . . . It was around three o'clock.'

Elisa suddenly fell silent. She swallowed. She frowned.

'I think I went out on that balcony to smoke,' she continued. 'Yeah, that was it. And then I saw this weird plastic bag down in the garden. It had been there a max of half an hour because I kept going out to smoke. I don't usually, but at parties I always feel like smoking.'

Again the same virtuous tone and role-playing mask. Lumikki would have admired the performance if it hadn't irritated her so much in this situation.

'What did you do then?' she asked, unable to restrain herself.

Elisa started fiddling with the golden heart dangling from the zipper of her pink jumpsuit. She pulled it down a couple of centimetres and then jerked it shut again. Open and shut. Open and shut. Lumikki drank a sip of coffee. It was painfully weak.

'For some reason I started laughing hysterically because it

just looked so weird sitting there in the snow. I can't explain it. I guess I was really wasted. I left the boys upstairs and went to get the bag. When I came inside, I opened it down there in the hall.'

Elisa swallowed again.

'At first I didn't understand what it was. I thought it was just rubbish. Then I pulled one of the pieces of paper out and realised it was money. Covered in blood. The whole plastic bag was full of blood-stained €500 notes. My hands got all bloody when I dug around in it. Thinking about it makes me sick. But then all I could do was laugh. Somehow it was just so ridiculously funny.'

Elisa stared at the pink rug on the black floor. The emotions on her face ran from nausea to disgust and from shame to fear.

'I didn't think at all about why the money was covered in blood. I yelled for the boys to come and look. They started laughing too and saying over and over that we're all fucking rich now. We didn't count it then, but the bag had €30,000 in it. We weren't actually thinking at all. Yeah, you know, except that we had to clean the money somehow.'

They had reasoned that they couldn't wash it at anyone's house since they wouldn't be able to get it dry without someone noticing. Then Tuukka came up with the school darkroom because he took photography. And he had a copy of his dad's key to the school he had made a long time ago. And he knew the code to the burglar alarm.

'It felt like the smartest idea in the world at the time,' Elisa explained, looking at Lumikki with pleading eyes. 'Can you understand?'

No, Lumikki thought, but she didn't say so out loud.

'And in the morning Tuukka had to hurry to get the money out of there,' she said instead.

'As far as I'm concerned, we should have left it there. I never wanted to touch it again. I can't help thinking where the blood came from. Was it from a person? And why was the bag in our garden? Who put it there? I'm never taking any fucking pills ever again. If I had been sober I might have seen who brought the bag.'

Elisa stood up and started pacing back and forth nervously.

Lumikki stood up as well, going to the balcony door and opening it. Cold air immediately assaulted her, but she didn't care. She went out on the balcony and looked down into the garden.

'Was that gate down there locked that night?' she asked.

'Yes,' Elisa replied. 'I checked it around two o'clock.'

Lumikki estimated the distance from the road to the garden. With a nice strong throw, it would be easy enough to toss a plastic rubbish bag over the stone fence.

'Is there a security camera on the street?'

Elisa shook her head.

'There is at the gate and at the door, but not on the street.'

Lumikki thought. She let the cold air nibble at her fingers. It kept her mind alert.

Someone had thrown a bag full of blood-soaked banknotes over the wall in the middle of the night. The money pointed to a payment. The blood pointed to a warning. So was the money a threat or a thank-you? And to whom? Had they thrown the bag into the right garden?

Viewed from the street, the house to the right looked very different, and the garden extended further out. The road made a small turn at Elisa's house, which was set further back.

'Who lives there?' Lumikki asked, indicating the house to the right.

'Two families with little kids. I think both mums are lawyers or something. One of the dads is some kind of artist and the other one works for the city. Their kids aren't in school yet.'

Lumikki sized up the duplex and garden. Confusing it with Elisa's family's house seemed unlikely. However, the house to the left, although clearly newer, was similar in size, shape and colour. Even the surrounding wall was an identical continuation of Elisa's family's. Someone could easily have mixed them up.

'And that one?'

Elisa was standing next to her shivering on the balcony now.

'Oh, him? He's a total weirdo. He's like forty or something, but he tries to look younger. It's like he's always living out some personal *Twilight* because he dresses in these long leather coats. He must think he looks like some kind of prince of the vampires or something. Really he just looks pathetic. I don't have a clue what he does. He works somewhere though, because every morning he goes out and then comes back at night. He lives alone in that big house, and I've never seen anyone visiting. He doesn't even say hi on the street.'

Lumikki looked at Elisa, whose eyes went wide.

'The money must have been meant for him! It just ended up in the wrong garden! Yeah, he's exactly the type to be mixed up in some dodgy deals or animal sacrifices or something.'

Elisa almost sounded pleased.

67

'That is one possibility,' Lumikki said. 'But not the only one.'

If the money had been thrown into the right garden, then the intended recipient was Elisa, her father or her mother.

Lumikki glanced at Elisa, whose teeth were beginning to chatter. She was like a stuffed animal, most of whose stuffing had fallen out, shivering in the cold. Hard to believe that she could be involved in anything that could result in a €30,000 pay-off. Although you never knew. Lumikki considered herself better than average at spotting liars. Elisa didn't seem like a liar. At least not a good enough one to be able to fool her. Lumikki had been lied to so many times in her life that she could pick out the changes in tone and expression that exposed the mediocre liar.

'Be that as it may, I have a bad feeling someone out there wants that money back. Right now,' Elisa whispered.

Lumikki had nothing comforting to say.

She agreed completely.

8

Viivo Tamm shivered. He couldn't remember the last time he had been so cold. He tried to bounce in place to keep warm, but his stiff leg muscles wouldn't cooperate.

He had only been standing at his guard post along the Pyynikki Hill running path for an hour, but he already felt as though he was coming up against the limits of what he could tolerate. He had on a thick parka with a tightly woven sweater underneath and a Thinsulate cap pulled down over his ears, but the cold was still finding a way though his layers. It attacked from even the smallest needle hole, mercilessly gnawing at his body, which was struggling desperately to maintain core temperature. Viivo Tamm decided to call.

Stiff fingers poked clumsily at the equally stiff buttons of the cell phone. He couldn't even consider removing his lined leather gloves. Extracting the correct name from the contact list and pressing the green 'call' icon took five minutes.

'Well?' came the expectant reply.

'Not a sign. And I can't stay out here much longer. I'm freezing to death.'

'Suck it up,' Boris Sokolov snapped and hung up.

Viivo stared at the phone for a second, clenching his teeth. Sokolov and Linnart Kask were sitting in a white van at the far end of the street. It was all well and good for them to be issuing orders sitting there all nice and toasty warm.

What if the girl didn't come out at all today? Or even just not very soon. All three of them knew they couldn't keep up the stakeout for hours on end. Someone would notice the van and get suspicious. Realise that no one around here needed a plumber right now. Switching the vehicle's licence plate and logos would cost time and money, and none of them wanted to do that any more than they had to.

Bloody, bloody hell. They had been sure that seeing the blood would be enough. But this guy had cooler nerves than they had thought. Now he was trying to play for higher stakes than he could afford though. Really he couldn't afford anything. None of them could. Not even Sokolov, even though he was happy to play the role of big bossman. But he was on just as tight a leash as the rest of them. A noose around the neck was still a noose even if it was encrusted with diamonds.

Maybe the Finn hadn't cared as much about the girl as they had thought after all. Maybe he had been acting. But kidnapping his daughter would snap him out of his delusions of grandeur.

Lumikki stared at the noodles in her bowl, which were a shade somewhere between grey and beige. Elisa had been telling the truth when she said she couldn't cook. Apparently the freezer held a supply of meals her mother had pre-made for her, but warming them up was 'such a hassle' that Elisa preferred to eat instant ramen. Lumikki sampled the limp strands floating

70

in the salty broth and decided to endure. Or actually, the low, steady growling of her stomach decided for her.

She was insanely hungry. Morning had turned to afternoon, and Lumikki's only thought was beginning to be when she was going to get home. Whenever she tried to start leaving, Elisa came up with some excuse why she had to stay. She really was afraid of being alone.

Their conversation was going nowhere. They had gone through everything related to the money. They had considered whether it was meant for the man in the leather coat next door. Elisa was convinced that it was.

'My mum and dad couldn't be mixed up in anything this weird. They're honest, upstanding citizens.'

Lumikki didn't think they could rule out the possibility that the money was meant for one of Elisa's parents. So she had asked what Elisa's mother did for work. Apparently she worked for a cosmetics company as part of a team that handled their international business. Not a big executive or anything, but Elisa said she earned a fair amount.

'She spends almost half her time travelling,' Elisa said, gazing out the window.

Lumikki saw a mixture of irritation and wistfulness in her face.

'Luckily Dad is almost always home,' Elisa continued, smiling. 'Except of course this last weekend.'

Elisa's dad, the police officer.

'What kind of policeman is your father?' Lumikki asked.

Elisa hung her head, mortified.

'Narcotics,' she replied.

The old saying about shoemaker's children going barefoot and all that. Lumikki would have been amused if she hadn't been so irritated by Elisa's stupidity. A narcotics officer's daughter playing around with illegal drugs. You'd think Elisa would know better than to take such risks. Lumikki didn't say anything, but Elisa interpreted her silence correctly.

'Come on, it's just occasional recreational use!' she said defensively. 'I'm not a junkie or anything. I know my limits. And I already said that I'm never going to use again. I'm straight edge from here on out.'

'You could probably ask your dad sometime how many "occasional recreational users" in this city have completely messed up their lives. But I didn't come here to lecture you about your drug habit. I'm just here to talk about the money.'

'I can't talk to Daddy about this though if he does have something dodgy going on,' Elisa said, sighing for the tenth time. 'Which of course I don't believe anyway. But if he did. Then I couldn't trust him. He could lie to me just as easily as anyone else. And I can't go to any other police because he's my dad. Even if he is mixed up in something, I can't betray him. And what if he's doing some undercover operation? God, my head is splitting!'

'What time does he come home today?' Lumikki asked.

'In a couple of hours.'

'Was he acting normally yesterday?'

'I think so. But I was so focused on hiding the fact that I had that party here and the elephant-sized secret in the back corner of my closet that I probably wouldn't have noticed if he had danced the polka wearing Mickey Mouse ears.'

'Pay attention. Talk to him. Don't ask directly, but see what his expressions and gestures reveal. People say an awful lot without ever opening their mouths,' Lumikki said. 'And keep an eye on that neighbour. If the money was meant for him, he's sure to start acting even weirder since he didn't get it.'

Elisa looked at her, stood up from the table, and walked over.

'Thanks,' Elisa said, hugging her quickly.

To Lumikki's astonishment, it didn't feel so unpleasant this time. Elisa returned to her chair and continued eating her noodles, sucking in her cheeks as she slurped them up and then drinking the broth from the bowl. Suddenly she looked like a little girl.

'I'll talk to Daddy. And spy on that neighbour. Maybe I'll find some perfectly logical explanation for all of this. And then I can think about what to do with the money. Tuukka and Kasper aren't going to like giving theirs up, but I can get them to fall in line if I want to,' Elisa said and smiled.

Something about her self-confidence was touching.

'Are you still afraid?' Lumikki asked.

'Not nearly as much.'

'Okay. Then I'm going home.'

Elisa tried a disappointed puppy-dog expression, but Lumikki stood firm. That was enough playing girlfriend for today. She had done her part.

Lumikki pulled on her coat, laced her combat boots up tight, and wrapped her scarf around her neck. She reached for her mittens on the hat shelf and then groped for her hat, which had slid further back. She had to stand up on her tiptoes to get a grip on the edge of it. Yanking, she heard an ominous sound.

'Oh no!' Elisa exclaimed as Lumikki pulled down her half-unravelled hat. 'There's still that set of hooks up there we haven't ever hung right. I've ripped a couple of things on it too.'

'Well, I guess I can wrap my scarf around my ears somehow,' Lumikki said.

'No, borrow one of my hats. I have plenty of them,' Elisa said, already pulling a red woollen cap down over Lumikki's head. 'I'll fix yours or just make you a new one.'

'Great. Okay. Thanks.'

Lumikki stood in the hall for a few more seconds. She felt as though there was something else encouraging she was supposed to say.

'Take care,' she finally said when she couldn't come up with anything else.

She wasn't good in the role of empathetic friend.

'Yeah,' Elisa said. 'If you want, you can go out through the back. Those front steps can get really slippery.'

She was biting her lip, looking as though she meant to say something more. Lumikki didn't ask what they would do next. She had a bad feeling this wouldn't be her last visit to Elisa's house.

Coming had been a mistake.

9

Boris Sokolov answered his cell phone before it could make it through the first bar of 'You Only Live Twice'.

'Well?'

'She just left through the back. Coming up the hill now,' Viivo Tamm said.

Sokolov nodded quickly to the Estonian sitting beside him, who started the van.

'Are you sure it's the right girl?' Boris asked.

'Yes. Same red hat as before,' Viivo replied.

'When you see us get close enough, run up on her. Don't say anything. We have to get her on the first try,' Boris said and hung up.

He rubbed his chilled hands to warm them up. They had to grab the girl and get her into the rear of the van instantly. No one could see. And the less the girl saw, the better. Not too rough though. She had to remain unharmed. But a couple of bruises wouldn't hurt. She had to think they were serious.

Because they were. Maybe in a slightly different way than she would think, but serious nonetheless.

Once they had her, they would send a video to her dear

daddy's cell phone. That would have to bring him to his senses. He would regret playing with the big boys. Boris hoped so anyway. That he would promise to play nice from now on. Agree to forget his next payment as a gesture of good will. Swear to do everything they thought to ask.

That would be enough.

Then they would let the girl out of the van and drive off to get the badges and licence plate switched. That was a big investment for one intimidation job, but in this case it would be worth the cost. Boris Sokolov had instructions from higher up, and they had promised to pay all the expenses plus a little extra thrown in. They couldn't afford to lose their inside man. But even more than that, he couldn't afford to lose them.

Of course the girl would run home to tell Daddy that the big bad men had kidnapped her. Her father would appear surprised and shocked, asking for details and descriptions, promising to file a police report and catch the bastards.

No, she wouldn't have to give any statement at the police station. Telling Daddy was enough. Daddy knew how traumatic an experience like that could be, and he didn't want to torment his daughter with an interrogation at the hands of strangers.

Boris almost laughed imagining the man trying to suppress his rage at not being able to tell anyone.

But he had made his bed and now he had to lie in it.

Lumikki decided to take the long way home over the hill. She had to get rid of the headache Elisa's perfume and asking so many questions had left her with. That the red knit cap seemed to be marinated in the same perfume didn't help the

76

situation at all. However, walking without a hat would have been a sure way to end up with frostbitten ears.

She remembered a year and a half earlier, just after moving to Tampere, coming to run on Pyynikki Hill for the first time. High on how free she was, she had sprinted the whole long, exhausting incline to the observation tower as fast as her legs would carry her. At the top, her legs were shaking and the smell of the fresh doughnuts they sold at the tower had screamed that she should just relax and call it a day. Why not sit down for some coffee and a sugar-coated treat? Lumikki continued her run, though, down past the tower, letting her running shoes fall lightly on the path. The shaking subsided and the joy of running returned.

The path took her back up a little and then, suddenly, to the left, an unbelievable view of Lake Pyhäjärvi opened up. Far off behind the old red-brick Pyynikki Tricot factory buildings, the low August sun caressed the water to the south. As she cut off the jogging path to the cliffs to take in the view, the green scents of late summer surrounded her. Gazing at the lake, Jalkasaari Island and the wooded suburbs of Tampere visible on the far shore, she felt completely happy. For the first time in a long time. Her own life started now. Freedom started now.

Now freedom and happiness were a distant memory. Lumikki tried not to think. Her thoughts just went in circles. No solution, no way out.

Or actually, there was one solution. The obvious, simple one. Go tell the police everything. Regardless of the trouble Elisa might end up in. Or her family might end up in. That wasn't her problem. But Elisa trusted her. Lumikki knew she couldn't betray that trust. Dead end.

Lumikki started walking up the road leading to the observation tower. Clouds obscured the sun. The light dimmed. The frosted white limbs of the trees crisscrossed in every direction. This forested hillside was straight from the pages of a fairy tale, but the shadows seemed as if they might conceal the most frightening creatures from those stories as well. Freakish beings fed by fear who snuck up behind you and pulled you into the snow, down to a cold, silent death. Or worse, turned a person into a living statue of ice unable to move or speak. Eternally living. Eternally dead.

Lumikki's breath steamed as she tried to exhale her thoughts, to empty her mind so new ideas could form. And she was just getting there when she realised someone was following her. Again. She didn't need to glance back to know that she was right.

But she looked anyway. The man walking behind her had pulled his skull cap down low and hiked up his scarf to cover his mouth and nose. Behind the man a white van moved along slowly, which was just pulling level with him.

Lumikki didn't think. She just ran, hearing the man behind her switch gears as well. Then the van sped up.

The frigid air tore at her lungs, and the soles of her combat boots slipped on the icy road. Lumikki managed to glance back just enough to see two men sitting in the van. They had also covered their faces, revealing only their eyes. Same gang.

No one was ahead of her. No one was to the sides. If she screamed, no one would hear.

Lumikki ran faster than she ever had in her life. The man

on foot fell behind, but the van caught up to her in seconds. The door opened and someone inside reached for Lumikki, managing to grab hold of something. Lumikki heard a ripping sound as the safety pin attaching her reflector to her coat sleeve tore a piece of fabric. Lumikki threw herself to the side, made a quick turn, and plunged off the road into the forest.

Jumping over rocks and mounds of snow, she wove between the trees, ignoring the branches that scratched her face. She heard the van's brakes squeal. She heard the men charge after her. She heard the shouts, which she guessed were Russian. She knew that the confusion her surprise turn had caused would only last so long. Lumikki knew that if they managed to surround her, she wouldn't stand a chance. She only had a few seconds' head start.

She had to use it right.

She wasn't going to get another chance.

Viivo Tamm swore as his leg once again sank into the snow. The girl seemed to know how to avoid the deepest drifts. Luckily her tracks showed where she had gone, even though he lost sight of her occasionally.

'Get her!' Boris yelled from further behind.

Get her yourself, fatso, Viivo would have liked to say. He sped up. The warmth was gradually beginning to return to his muscles, and their ability to accept instructions was improving with every step. He was going to catch the little bitch. *You can run, but you can't hide. Running in the snow is going to start wearing you down too.* Viivo might not have been the fastest, but he had endurance.

Just now he couldn't see the girl. The tracks led out of the thicket onto a lit walking path. She probably hoped that some random jogger would happen along and save her. Not a chance. No one in their right mind went out for a jog in temperatures like this. Viivo glanced left and right.

The girl was gone. Bloody, bloody hell.

Then he saw something red further down the path. The girl's hat.

It had fallen off, left behind like a signpost. Poor Little Red Riding Hood. Leaving such clear signs for the Big, Bad Wolf wasn't a good idea. Boris and Linnart were just rumbling out of the forest. Viivo was already running in the direction indicated by the cap and yelled for them to follow. The girl couldn't be far off.

Lumikki watched from a tree limb, pressed against the trunk, as the three men ran in the wrong direction. She had run onto the path and leapt to the tree, leaving as few marks as possible in the snow, and shimmied up. Then she had hurled the hat as far as she could down the path.

It had worked. But it wouldn't fool them for long.

Ignoring the painful jolt to the soles of her feet as she dropped to the ground, she took off running again. Now the frozen air savaged her ears along with her lungs. But she barely felt it.

Away. Escape. Back to the road where the delivery van stood parked. The side said Mäkinen HVAC. Lumikki would have bet anything that none of the men were named Mäkinen. She memorised the plate number, even though she guessed it wouldn't be any use.

Her heart was pounding in her ears.

Off the hill back onto Pyynikki Road. Now she started seeing cars and people. The lights of an approaching bus were the most beautiful thing she had ever seen. Lumikki hailed the bus from a distance and the driver took pity on her running in the cold and pulled off before the stop. Panting, Lumikki climbed on, paid her fare, and took the nearest free seat.

Her legs were trembling. Breathing hurt. As warm air flowed into her cold-punished lungs, an uncontrollable coughing fit racked her body.

The old lady sitting across from her gave her a simultaneously sympathetic and disapproving look.

'You should think about wearing some sort of hat in weather like this, young lady,' she said helpfully. 'Otherwise you'll catch your death.'

Lumikki coughed in reply. Feeling began returning to her ears as a tingling itch. She pressed her hands to her ears to transfer body heat from her palms. What the hell had just happened? Why had someone just tried to kidnap her? If it had just been an attempted rape, it seemed strange that the men continued pursuing her so manically. They had to have some connection to the money. But why had they wanted Lumikki, who was little more than a random, unlucky bystander?

'A woollen cap would be best,' the old woman said, continuing her sermon.

The hat. The red knitted cap. In that moment Lumikki realised that the men hadn't been chasing her at all. They had been chasing a girl in a red hat. And who did the red hat really belong to? Exactly. They had wanted Elisa. Of course.

81

That made much more sense. But unfortunately, that meant there was no longer any doubt about the money having been thrown in the correct garden. The pursuit of a girl believed to be Elisa confirmed it.

Lumikki considered what would have happened had Elisa left the house wearing the red hat instead of her. Understanding hit her in the gut. Elisa never would have got away. Elisa would be in that van right now, helpless, a prisoner, at the mercy of her hunters. Lumikki quickly pulled out her phone and texted Elisa.

Whatever you do, don't leave the house. Keep the doors locked. Don't let anyone in you don't know.

WEDNESDAY, 2 MARCH

Once upon a time there was a girl who was not afraid.

The girl ran as people run who do not fear falling. Her small, strong, nimble feet sped over the rocks and stumps. On the soles of her feet she felt the soft moss, the sun-warmed sand, the prickly pine needles, the dewy grass. She trusted that her legs would carry her wherever she wished to go.

The girl laughed as those laugh who have not yet known humiliation. Her laughter started deep in her belly. It filled her chest, gurgled in her throat, and bubbled on her tongue. Finally it wriggled out of her mouth, shot through the air, and burst into apple blossoms on the trees. Her laughter warmed and brightened all that surrounded her. Often it ended in hiccupping, but that did not matter because the hiccupping only made her laugh all the more.

The girl trusted as those trust for whom the earth has never given way, whom no one has ever betrayed. She hung head-down and trusted that she would not fall. Or if she fell, someone would catch her before she hit the ground.

Once upon a time there was a girl who learned to fear.

Fairy tales do not begin this way. Other, darker stories do.

10

Lumikki was little again. She was nine years old. Or ten. Or twelve. In that hell the years ran together, sliding forward interlocked as one black, indeterminate mass. Distinguishing or remembering what had happened when was impossible. What was real and what nightmare.

But one thing she did know. She had never been afraid for no reason.

Lumikki curled up as small as possible and listened. She knew how to squeeze into an incredibly small space. She fitted in cabinets. She fitted in the dark, cluttered corners of closets. She fitted into flat spaces no one ever thought to look. She knew how to be so quiet that normal breathing would have sounded like a hammer drill in comparison.

Her nose ran. She let it run, controlling the overwhelming urge to sniff or wipe it with a sleeve. Thin, almost water-like snot ran onto her lips. She did not lick. The mucus continued its way down to her jaw and then dripped onto her knee. It had no significance. Her jeans were already dirty in any case. Mum would wonder about it at home. Mum would wonder, and she would keep her mouth shut tight.

There were things best not talked about.

There were things that only got worse if you said them out loud.

Lumikki listened. She heard the steps as they approached. She concentrated on them in order to stay calm. If she gave power to the fear, staying quiet would be impossible. She closed her eyes and thought of untouched, freshly fallen snow. She imagined a blue twilight. She made a rabbit bound across the snow, leaving beautiful, uniform tracks. Two small circles, one in front of the other, then two oblong marks side by side. The tracks calmed her nerves.

Nothing bad can happen once the rabbit has run safely across the snow.

Nothing bad can happen with the first stars appearing in the sky.

Nothing bad can happen with a snug cottage just a few steps away and the porch lamp burning brightly. Lumikki listened as the steps retreated. She breathed a little more freely.

She had succeeded in staying hidden. She had not been found out.

How would it feel not to need to be afraid every day?

Lumikki did not wake up with a start. She shifted gradually from sleeping to wakefulness, feeling her legs and arms growing, her body changing from a girl's to a woman's, uncoiling from a ball. She accepted the years that separated her from the Lumikki of her dreams. She was not small any more. She was seventeen. And she hadn't needed to be afraid every day for ages now.

Except she was again. Because she had gone and meddled in someone else's affairs.

Elisa had been calling her all night, hysterical, jumping at every squeak and crack of the cold house, wanting to hear Lumikki's reassuring words. She had panicked when her father didn't come home when he said he would. In the middle of one call, Elisa suddenly shrieked. After that, Lumikki listened as Elisa ran somewhere, slammed a door behind her, and snapped the lock shut.

'Someone just came through the front door,' Elisa croaked, returning to the phone.

'Okay. Where are you now?'

'I locked myself in the bathroom.'

Lumikki had surmised as much from the sounds. Apparently Elisa did not know how to move silently. She had never needed to learn. If a professional killer had forced his way into the house, the noise she was making would lead him to her instantly. And besides, a locked bathroom was probably the worst possible hiding place. She would be like a microwavable TV dinner in there. All you had to do was use enough force to open the packaging and then devour the contents. You didn't even really have to heat it up.

'Did whoever it is break through the door?' Lumikki had asked.

'No, they used a key.'

Lumikki had felt like hanging up right then and there. Instead of waiting around for Elisa's next sentence, which was beyond predictable even before she opened her mouth.

'Huh. Maybe it's my dad. Yeah, he's calling me from downstairs,' Elisa had whispered into the phone.

No shit, Sherlock.

'Good. I'm hanging up now,' Lumikki had said firmly.

'Don't go! Or, I mean, not before you promise to come again tomorrow. I can't be here alone, and I can't go anywhere else.'

Elisa's voice had a surprising strength.

Lumikki had wanted to refuse. She had wanted to be done with the whole mess while it was still possible to get out. Her pursuers hadn't got a good look at her. She could still wash her hands of this. They weren't really even dirty yet. She wasn't the one who dove into a bag of blood-stained money with both hands.

Lumikki felt like banging her head against the wall after ending the call. She had gone and promised Elisa she'd come. Again.

Boris Sokolov drummed his fingers against the side of his beer glass. The drink was flat and foul-tasting. An excellent fit for his mood. The first beer-hungry bar maggots had crawled out of their holes and were already sitting in the dimly lit room at their regular tables. Boris had reserved a booth for himself and the Estonians. By all appearances no one had bothered to wipe down the table at the end of the night shift. And why should they bother? That fitted his mood perfectly too.

They had botched it. Pulled a Russkie, the Finns sitting at their usual tables would say, and this time Boris wouldn't be able to argue. They had to abandon the kidnapping plan. They'd had one chance, one try, and now they had wasted it. Boris had received a short text message simply saying that he needed to handle the job. He was personally responsible.

He had to come up with some other way to get this guy scared back into line.

'What if he doesn't realise Natalia is dead?' Viivo Tamm suggested, following the question with a long pull from his glass.

'He has to know. Who else's blood would he think was on the money?' Boris asked.

Viivo shrugged. Linnart Kask said nothing. Sometimes Boris suspected Linnart was even simpler than he let on.

Boris considered Viivo's words. Could there be something to that? What if the cop really didn't understand that his beloved Natalia was a corpse? Natalia might not have told him about her plan to escape with the money. Right now the cop might just be irritated that he had to deal with a bunch of cash with stains all over it. Maybe that was why he was claiming he hadn't received it at all.

Boris had thought the cop and Natalia genuinely cared about each other. He had been sure that they had drawn up her getaway plan together. Perhaps he had underestimated Natalia's ability to make her own decisions. Natalia might have finally realised that it didn't pay to trust anyone too much and that no one was going to save her. On some level Boris understood Natalia's decision.

He had never said it to Natalia, but at times he had thought of her as the daughter he never had. A small part of Boris had wanted to let Natalia escape. But a larger part of him had understood the scale of the trouble he would have been causing himself if he had. That was why he'd had to harden his feelings and think of Natalia running across the snow as a rabbit. Just a common pest. Only then had he been able to pull the trigger.

But even if the cop hadn't known about Natalia's plan, that didn't remove their current problem. That he was trying to shake them down. That they had to put a stop to it, and fast.

Browsing the calendar on his phone was Boris's way of trying to calm his nerves. Usually it worked. Now it gave him an idea.

'I think Natalia is going to send our policeman an invitation to a party soon,' he said with a smile.

The Estonians looked at him in astonishment. *Boneheads.* Boris felt as if he had the only brain in their troika. Luckily it was a good one. Leaving the rest of the swill in his glass, he went to the bar to order a double whisky. He had earned it.

Lumikki almost turned round and left when she saw the two extra pairs of shoes in the entryway. Size forty-one and size forty-three, in men's. She didn't remember agreeing to come to a secret meeting of the Grumpy, Sleepy and Dopey club.

'Let's go over one more time what exactly I'm doing here, since apparently Tuukka and Kasper are here too,' Lumikki said to Elisa, who stared at her feet, embarrassed.

Feet wearing pink-and-black striped socks, of course.

'Well, see . . . you're the only one who knows how to fix this. Since you're so smart,' Elisa said.

The boot-licking unctuous voice and accompanying sickly-sweet smile backfired. Lumikki started pulling her combat boots back on.

'I thought I was coming because you were scared and alone. No, because you demanded that I come. Because you can't be alone. Well. You clearly aren't alone any more. Case closed. Now I can go.'

Elisa slipped between Lumikki and the door.

'You can't go now. Tuukka and Kasper forced their way in

91

after they realised I wasn't at school. They didn't believe me when I said I had a migraine. I can't get through this without you,' Elisa pleaded.

Lumikki's fingers fiddled with the laces of her boots for a few seconds.

She had promised herself she wasn't going to be afraid any more. She had only been thinking of herself then though. She hadn't thought that she could be afraid for someone else. If she left now and closed the door behind her, she might get herself out of all of this. She wouldn't be getting away from the fear though. She could ignore Elisa's calls and text messages. She could even get an unlisted number. She could avoid seeing Elisa at school. She could treat her like she was air.

But she couldn't stop herself from thinking. She couldn't stop herself from contemplating what could happen to Elisa and whether the men who chased Lumikki might get their hands on her eventually. She would be afraid on Elisa's behalf. She didn't want that.

Lumikki knew she was already in deep, in over her combat boots. It was all the same now whether she sank in up to her knees or her waist or her neck.

In hot water. Up shit creek. Not free. Lumikki hated that. But she couldn't do anything about it.

Sighing deeply, she began pulling off her boots.

'I'll stay. But just so you know, if Tuukka tries his tough-guy routine again, I'm calling the police that very second and throwing you all to the wolves.'

Elisa clapped her hands enthusiastically. Lumikki might as well have been listening to her own death knell.

11

'Did you find anything out from your dad last night?' Tuukka asked Elisa as she brought them large glasses of Coke in the living room.

Kasper had asked for his with a kick, but Elisa's expression wiped the grin off his face.

Lumikki glanced at Tuukka. Elisa must have told the boys everything. Blabbermouth. But maybe it was best this way. Talking would be easier if they were all looking at the same map.

'My brain was barely functioning I was so hysterical about those men chasing Lumikki. I mean, chasing her thinking she was me. In the state I was in, I was lucky I could keep my mouth shut, let alone pull off some cunning secret interrogation.'

Elisa set down the serving tray with the Coke glasses on the living-room table. Ice cubes clinked against each other. She looked even more tired than she had the day before. The circles under her eyes were darker, her hair hadn't been washed, and she didn't have any make-up on. She was like a stain on the pure linen fabric of the stylish living room, a blotch on one of the designer furnishings that oozed Boknäs and Artek. From the ceiling hung a large bulbous lamp made of thin strips of wood laminate. Scandinavian lines, elegant artlessness, all for a price.

Lumikki found herself wondering again how they could pay for all of this on the salaries of a police officer and cosmetics sales agent. No one on the police force was making bank, and Elisa's mum's salary couldn't be all that astronomical either. An inheritance? Perhaps.

Or maybe it had something to do with a plastic bag full of blood-stained money.

'Okay. Next, let's check your mum and dad's computers,' Kasper said with the self-assurance of an up-and-coming small-time hood.

'Mum took her laptop with her on her trip, but Dad's computer is in his office over there. But I don't know –'

Elisa didn't manage to complete her sentence before Kasper was already marching to the office door.

'I'll check the computer. You guys check the files and stuff,' Kasper said.

Lumikki, Tuukka, and Elisa followed him into the office.

'Isn't this sort of illegal?' Elisa asked as she riffled through her father's desk drawers.

'I don't remember legality really being much of an obstacle for you before,' Tuukka said with a laugh.

Elisa sighed. 'Maybe it should be.'

Lumikki agreed, but she didn't say so. Instead she voiced another concern.

'We aren't going to find anything about your dad's work here. He's got to have super-strict rules about what papers he can bring home. Probably none. And the computer is a home computer. All of his work things are going to be on his work computer.'

'True. How did I not remember that?'

'Let's look anyway,' Tuukka insisted. 'There's no way he would store anything about crimes he's committing at work. That place is crawling with snitches.'

Elisa's scowl limited Tuukka's smile to that faint upturning at the corner of his mouth. They searched in silence, without result. The office didn't reveal anything but a meticulous father who kept his tax returns, insurance policies and bills organised and the folders on his computer clean.

'He hasn't even been looking at any porn sites,' Kasper grumbled impatiently.

'Yuck! Of course he hasn't.' Elisa shuddered.

'But you have,' Tuukka snickered. 'I've done enough snooping around your computer to know that.'

'Once, maybe, when a friend sent a link, and I clicked on it without thinking,' Elisa objected.

Lumikki couldn't stand listening to the trio's pointless blather. What irritated her the most was Elisa's voice, which around the boys had turned shrill, and her comments, which were growing increasingly stupid. Lumikki knew the phenomenon. All through middle school she had watched in bewilderment as it took hold. After the summer between sixth and seventh grades, some of the girls came back to school acting as though they had dropped half of their brains in a lake somewhere. Girls who used to be so smart suddenly couldn't even do simple maths or run a hundred-metre dash without complaining they were 'going to die'.

'Seriously, I'm gonna die!' they would squeal over and over throughout the day, sometimes thrilled, sometimes feigning helplessness. They painted their eyes and snapped bubble gum. Figuring out that the girls' stupid act was meant for the boys had taken Lumikki some time. That their behaviour was a signal that they were small, cute and harmless. And sexy in just the right way for certain boys.

They shrank and dumbed themselves down so the best-looking boys in class could feel smarter and stronger. Lumikki had always wondered why the boys couldn't see through the act. Didn't they find it humiliating that the girls thought they had to pretend so the boys could feel superior? Some of them did see behind the mask, but the show wasn't directed at them. They were too smart to be sexy.

For some reason intelligence wasn't sexy in middle school. If you wanted to be sexy, you had to avoid intelligence like the plague. Smart meant the same thing as boring, annoying, irritating and, if not actually ugly, at least nothing to talk about.

Lumikki had thought things would change after middle school. Partly they did, but partly not. Now she saw that even some really accomplished adult women still dumbed themselves down in male company. It was embarrassing to watch. She hoped Elisa just had one foot still stuck in junior high and that the behaviour was a result of that and not some deeper trait or ingrained pattern.

'Let me take a look at the computer for a sec too,' Lumikki said to Kasper.

Kasper looked at her dubiously. 'There isn't anything there,' he said.

'Just let me look anyway,' Lumikki insisted calmly. 'Sometimes machines have eaten a lot more than it looks like on the surface.'

'Ooo, so our super detective is also some kind of fucking computer genius,' Tuukka said mockingly.

'Yeah. I'm the secret love child of Hercule Poirot and Lisbeth Salander,' Lumikki replied without the slightest wavering in her expression and sat down in front of the computer in the place Kasper had just vacated dramatically.

The trio stood behind her watching. Lumikki hated that.

'So you're Lumikki Poisander then?' Kasper asked, trying to keep up the joke.

No one laughed.

'Lumikki, Lumikki.'

Kasper seemed to be savouring the name, drawing out each syllable.

'You must have a nickname,' he said finally.

'No, I don't,' Lumikki replied without turning around.

'Lumi?'

'No.'

'Mikki?'

'You think?'

'Okay, maybe not. What about Snow White then?'

Lumikki pushed back the office chair so suddenly that the backrest ran into Kasper and then spun it around.

'Ouch! Watch it.' Kasper massaged his knee irritably.

'Chill out. This could take a while,' Lumikki said, throwing Elisa a significant look.

Fortunately, the girl still used her brain sometimes.

'Let's go finish our Cokes in the living room,' Elisa said. 'Shout if you find anything.'

Lumikki nodded and turned back to the monitor. After a moment, she heard the door close behind her. Blessed quiet.

She had to act quickly. No way would the quiet last.

12

Terho Väisänen turned up his collar and pulled the green scarf his daughter had knitted him over his mouth. The cold sank its sharp claws into any bare patch of skin as soon as he stepped outside. He considered running home from the police station to Pyynikki by car but decided to walk after all. Maybe the cold would stimulate his brain, which had been unacceptably sluggish.

Two questions were bothering Terho.

Where was his money?

Where was Natalia?

And was that the order of importance of those questions? Of course not, but sometimes Natalia went quiet for several days on end, sometimes even weeks. She didn't always have time to answer Terho's calls and texts and emails. He was used to that. So it didn't really mean anything yet. What it did mean though was that Boris Sokolov had practically reached through the cell phone to throttle Terho when he called to ask about the money. Sokolov said the money had been delivered.

But it hadn't.

Either Sokolov was lying or the Estonians were lying to

Sokolov. The latter was more likely. Terho had actually been surprised that they had gone so long without someone trying to stick their hand in the cookie jar and make some quick cash. He chalked this discipline up to the Estonians having seen how Sokolov dealt with disloyalty. No one wanted to experience Sokolov's brand of justice. And like everyone else, Sokolov took his orders from higher up. The hierarchy of power and fear kept everyone in line.

Except for now. Someone had decided to take a little extra for himself.

Terho hated the thought that a system that had worked so well up until now might be breaking apart. He had done his own part without questioning it. From the beginning he was in this for the money, and he still needed that. If the cash stopped coming, his options would be limited. He hadn't built himself a safety buffer for the future, even though he knew he should have. The amount he had in savings was paltry. Of course he could always burn Sokolov and company in revenge, but that was impossible without implicating himself to boot. All that would be left was smoking wreckage.

He couldn't let that happen.

Because negotiations hadn't gone anywhere with Sokolov, he would have to try making an agreement directly with Polar Bear. That wouldn't be easy. Polar Bear wrote his own rules, and if he didn't like the way the game was going, he simply knocked the other players off the board.

Terho walked along the Tampere Highway and cursed himself for ever having got involved. Not only was it criminal, it was morally wrong. It was, no matter how many mornings he had spent staring out the window while his family still slept, rationalising how the arrangement had its good sides. For the police force and for the community. He had received information from Sokolov that had helped the police capture any number of dealers and traffickers. They had cleaned up the Tampere underworld so thoroughly that Terho's unit had received commendations from the highest levels of government. Terho had reminded himself of that as he watched the neighbouring homes waking from their morning slumber. The slowly rising sun had mocked his self-deception though. He had to avert his gaze from the sun, pour more milk in his coffee and look elsewhere as he continued lying to himself.

Back then, years ago, taking the offer had seemed like the only viable option. Gaming debts and unpaid loans hung around his neck. Terho had drifted imperceptibility into a downward spiral of gambling. At first gambling had been an easy way to relax and clear his head after a hard day at work, but little by little it became a full-blown addiction. Playing online especially was far too easy. And he had to play for money so it would feel like something, so he could get the adrenaline rush he needed. He had also had a wife at home with expensive tastes, and at that point Terho had still wanted to give her all the best the world could offer. And of course his daughter, whom he loved more than he had ever thought possible.

It was also for Elisa. Everything he had done had also been for her. So she would never have to be ashamed of her house or her clothes. Or ever wonder if they would have enough for what they wanted. Too often as a child and teenager, Terho had been forced to lie that a pair of flea-market jeans were actually new or that a coat from his cousin was really from a trip they took abroad. Their middle-class income had gone down his father's throat. Terho had been so ashamed of that he'd become a teetotaller and joined the narcotics force, since there was nothing he could do about the deadly drug named alcohol.

Nevertheless, a tendency for addiction had apparently been passed from father to son. The need to get kicks from something, fast and without a lot of thought. But Terho had always made sure his gaming didn't interfere with his family. It was his private, personal vice. He had even succeeded in cutting down how much he played compared to his worst addict years, but that still didn't mean he could get along without a regular fix.

For the past year, one of the reasons Terho had continued to cooperate with Sokolov was Natalia. Despite how much younger she was, he was helplessly in love, head-over-heels, like a teenager. He had known from the beginning that it was crazy and hopeless and dangerous, but he could never resist Natalia's smile and those big, innocent eyes you would never guess had seen so much. He was already mourning the fact that at some point he would be forced to give up Natalia's company, her silky smooth skin and the dimples in her cheeks. It was unavoidable. The relationship couldn't continue unless Terho was willing to sacrifice his marriage, his family and ultimately his career for it. He wasn't ready for that, despite having told her in tender moments that he would leave his wife and begin a new life with her. The promises of a man in love that he could never keep. Natalia understood well enough. She was a smart young woman, smarter than she looked.

But Terho wanted to arrange things for her. He at least owed her that much. He wanted Natalia to have a better life and not have to work for Sokolov any more. Terho didn't know how he would handle it yet, but he trusted that he would come up with something. That was another reason the whole thing couldn't fall apart right now just because the Estonians couldn't keep their fingers to themselves.

In the park, a painfully cold wind was coming in off the lake, making Terho start to regret that he hadn't taken a car. Even the state-of-the-art technology of his Haglöfs coat was no match for this insanely cold winter.

A meeting had fallen through, suddenly leaving him a good hour of extra time. He had decided to use it to stop by at home and make lunch for himself and Elisa, who was suffering from a migraine or some women's complaint. Or plain old laziness. Terho had to admit that to himself. His daughter was sweet and popular and the dearest thing to him in the world, but she wasn't the brightest bulb on the string of Christmas lights. Maybe high school wasn't really the place for her after all.

Terho considered his plan.

He would have to contact Polar Bear. The only way would be via email and sending the email would only work from his home computer, because he didn't dare take the risk at work or on his phone browser.

At the same time he could send Natalia another email and ask why he hadn't heard from her. He missed her so much. The longing chilled his bones even more than the biting wind.

Brown eyes. Bleached hair, with just a hint of darker roots.

Here and there streaks lighter than the rest. Hair extensions. Thin, plucked eyebrows. Lips that might be enhanced or might just be that full naturally.

Age: somewhere between seventeen and twenty-five?

In most of her pictures she struck a serious pose, lips slightly parted. In one picture she was smiling though, showing off her deep dimples. When she smiled she looked younger and more open. In the same picture was a middle-aged man who had exactly the same nose as Elisa. The woman wore expensive clothing that announced just how expensive it was. There was one more close-up of the couple, probably taken themselves with a camera phone, that showed them kissing and laughing. They looked obscenely happy.

Lumikki felt like a voyeur looking at the pictures, which had been hidden rather primitively on the computer. Before finding them she had already located a username and password for an anonymous email account. The mail folders were empty though. Elisa's dad either didn't use it or – more likely – he always deleted any emails after reading them.

'Elisa!' Lumikki called.

Elisa came to the door. Mercifully Tuukka and Kasper had decided to entertain themselves by playing Wii in the living room.

'Will you close the door, please?' Lumikki asked and Elisa complied. Then Lumikki continued.

'I'm assuming the woman in these pictures isn't your mum.'

13

Elisa wrapped her arms around herself. Suddenly she was cold. She wanted to close her eyes and not see the pictures, but even that wouldn't have helped. They were already burned deep into her brain and would still be running on her internal movie screen that night when she closed her eyes and tried to sleep.

How could Daddy do this to her? And to her mum?

Elisa wasn't stupid. For a long time she had known her parents' relationship wasn't happy in a romantic sense and that they were mostly still together out of habit and convenience. Still, it felt inconceivable to think that Daddy had cheated on her mum. Daddy wasn't like that. Daddy was honest and honourable and dependable. Daddy was the kind of man who got divorced first before starting anything new with anyone. Actually, Elisa hadn't been so sure about her mum. Elisa wouldn't have been surprised to learn that her mum didn't always spend her nights alone when she was travelling for work. More than plausible, she thought it was probable.

But Daddy. With a younger woman, barely older than Elisa herself. The whole idea made her sick. Even worse than the relationship was the secrecy and the lying, the lack of trust.

If it was even a real relationship. It could just be . . . But why would Daddy have kept the pictures on his computer then? They had to mean something, because he wanted to be able to look at them again.

'Maybe . . .'

Elisa heard Lumikki's voice as if in a dream. What if this was all a dream and she could wake up . . . right . . . now!

Suddenly the door flew open and Tuukka and Kasper tumbled in.

'Important girl talk going on in here? Or has our computer whiz actually found something? Woo-hoo.'

Lumikki felt awkward having Elisa, Kasper and Tuukka staring over her shoulder at the pictures. The worst thing about it was being able to sense Elisa's embarrassment without even turning around.

'Maybe she's just . . . or I mean maybe Daddy's just . . .' she said, trying desperately to articulate some kind of explanation.

'Let's face it,' Kasper said. 'Your dad is banging some young chick.'

All of their thoughts spoken aloud. Perhaps not word for word, but the content was the same.

'There could be some other explanation for these pictures,' Elisa said feebly.

Lumikki could hear from her voice that Elisa knew Kasper was right.

'I'd bet anything this has something to do with the money,' Tuukka said. 'Two secrets like this at once can't be a coincidence.'

'But how?' Elisa asked.

'Doesn't she look a little bit Russian?' Kasper asked. 'Maybe

105

she's a who— sorry, I mean prostitute. Maybe your dad is mixed up in some kind of sex business.'

Elisa shook her head. Looking at her now, Lumikki realised she was on the verge of tears.

'Or maybe . . .' Tuukka was going to take a stab at speculating now.

But just then the computer pinged to signal the arrival of a new email. Lumikki had left the anonymous email account open in the browser just in case something interesting happened to come in.

Bull's eye.

The sender was using an anonymous account too. The handle 'Beautifulrose' and a top-level domain name didn't reveal much. Lumikki read the message out loud. It was written in English.

My love,

I had to create another email address. Just to be careful. Polar Bear is having a party on Friday. Wants you to be there. And so do I :). There will be a black car picking you up at 8 p.m. Because the theme is fairy tales and because I know what you like, I'm going as the Snow Queen. I've got something important to tell you.

Kisses, N

P.S. Please delete this message right after reading as always. We have to be extra careful.

Tuukka, Kasper and Elisa glanced at each other.

'What the hell does that mean?' Elisa asked.

'Polar Bear, Polar Bear . . .' Kasper repeated. 'Oh my God. Polar Bear. Your dad just got an invitation to one of Polar Bear's parties.'

'Where? Whose party?'

'Polar Bear's!' Kasper almost yelled. 'He's a legend. I mean, I don't know much more than that he's some kind of super big shot who basically everyone respects. I've heard he runs all kinds of different legal and illegal businesses and basically no one has ever seen him. The rumours about his parties are really wild. Apparently he has some kind of crazy mansion or castle where he hosts these off-the-hook blowouts. Everybody goes. I mean everybody who's rich and important.'

'What is this Polar Bear guy's real name?' Lumikki asked.

Kasper looked at her in amusement. 'How should I know? You'd have to be a serious insider to know something like that.'

'So he's like a mob boss or something?' Elisa had instinctively lowered her voice.

Kasper spread his arms. 'Well, I doubt he'd want the cops to know about all of his businesses. But what do I know? He's so rich and clever that he never gets caught. He never gets his own hands dirty.'

'How do you know so much?' Tuukka asked.

A satisfied smile appeared on Kasper's lips. Lumikki could see that Kasper thought he had one up on the rest of them.

'I have my sources. When you spend time on the street you hear things. And don't bother asking any more. I get you guys pills, and I get you information. That's all you need to know.'

While the others were talking, Lumikki copied the email down word for word on a slip of paper that she then shoved in her trouser pocket.

'Be that as it may, we have to trash this email,' she said. 'Unfortunately it says that it's been opened once already now,

107

so your dad will know that someone has been in his account.'

Lumikki prepared to delete the message.

Terho Väisänen's fingers were frozen through even though his gloves were supposed to be Windstopper fabric with all kinds of insulating layers. He tried to get his joints flexible enough to get the key into the front-door lock.

He remembered the previous December. When it was only a couple of degrees below freezing with snow falling so gently you almost didn't notice it. He had been standing with Natalia by a light sculpture in Tampella. The sculpture radiated a blue light that made Natalia's face look unreal.

They had just been for coffee. The new housing development on the river was relatively safe. No one he knew lived there. Neither his wife nor Elisa had any reason to visit. Only people who lived in the area should be around, since it wasn't on the way to anywhere. There weren't any shops or restaurants that would attract people to go out of their way. The coffee shop was just barely scraping by on the euros local residents brought in. In Tampella they dared to appear in public together. Even though there were still risks.

Sometimes you had to take a risk. And besides, the fear of getting caught added to the thrill. Of course Terho had a cover story in case a friend or a friend of a friend happened to see them together. He could always point to his work, intelligence gathering and the importance of confidentiality. He could make them think that Natalia was giving him information but that he couldn't reveal any more than that. Hush-hush. Terho was relieved he had never been forced to use his cover story yet.

108

Natalia had forgotten her gloves. She blew on her small hands. Terho took them between his own to warm them up. Natalia smiled. Snowflakes stuck to her hair. They also reflected the blue light of the statue. Natalia was wearing a white coat and white boots. She looked more beautiful than she ever had before.

'My snow queen,' Terho breathed into her ear.

Suddenly an intense desire hit him to warm Natalia all over, to press his burning palms against her cool skin, to melt every flake of snow.

'Let's go,' he said hoarsely and pulled Natalia along, quickening his steps. In five minutes they were at the reception desk of Hotel Tammer. They got a room. He made a quick call to his wife informing her that he would be working overtime late into the night. Then he turned back to Natalia, who didn't look so much like a fairy-tale creature any more in the warm yellow light of the hotel room. That didn't matter though. The mental image had already created the desire. Pulling Natalia to him, he closed his eyes.

Terho Väisänen returned to the present, clumsy fingers fiddling with his key, and uttered a string of curses.

Lumikki heard the sounds first.

In a hushed voice, she said, 'Someone's coming.'

Elisa jumped.

'The men who chased you! The killers!'

Lumikki restrained her desire to slap her hand over Elisa's mouth. Did she really have such an underdeveloped sense of self-preservation? Did living in a pink-and-black room pickle your brain and turn your thoughts to mush?

109

'Let's just stay calm and keep quiet. Obviously whoever it is has a key. I'm guessing it's your dad. The most important thing is that we don't let him know that we were in here by making too much noise.'

As she spoke, Lumikki calmly deleted the email, logged out of the account, closed the secret picture folder and browser window, and then turned off the machine. To Lumikki it felt as if each step took an agonisingly long time. She knew she was just imagining that though. In reality it all happened in a matter of seconds.

Then again, it also only took seconds for the person at the door to get the key into the lock and click it open.

'Go. Upstairs.'

Lumikki issued her command as quietly as possible. It was enough to convince Elisa, Tuukka and Kasper, who slipped out of the study and rushed to the stairs. They probably thought they were being quiet, but to Lumikki their exit sounded like a herd of wildebeests who had just heard a lion roar.

Turn off already. Turn off.

The computer stayed stuck at the 'Shutting down . . .' screen for too long. Lumikki guessed that the machine had the same problem her own laptop did, that occasionally it just refused to power down for no particular reason.

She heard the door open. Fortunately the front door did not have a direct line of sight to the office. Someone large stepped into the house. A man.

Lumikki controlled her breath, concentrating on keeping her pulse in check. Then she firmly pressed the computer's power button and held it down. The next time it booted up, the machine might complain about not being shut down properly, which could arouse Elisa's father's suspicion, but now her only option was to take that risk. Most likely he would act just like anyone else and wonder for two seconds about why the machine had crashed, then shrug and start thinking about buying a new one soon.

Turn off already.

The screen went black.

'Elisa! I decided to come home for lunch! I'll make some food,' he shouted up the stairs.

Good. Lumikki had been right.

Quietly she hid behind the office door, hoping fervently that Elisa's dad wouldn't come in there first.

She could hear him taking off his cold-weather clothes. Then his steps approached the office.

Go past.

He was already continuing past into the kitchen, but then changed his mind and stepped into the room. Lumikki held her breath. She was flat. She was odourless. She did not exist.

Don't sit down. Lumikki knew that the chair would still be warm.

Elisa's dad did not sit. Standing at the desk, he sorted the mail. Lumikki still held her breath. She knew she could keep calm holding her breath for at least two minutes. Elisa's dad tossed a couple of envelopes, presumably bills, towards the back corner of the desk. Then he headed back out to the kitchen.

'What do you want? Should I make some pasta? Or maybe that chicken curry soup you like? I've got to have something hot after freezing my soul outside.'

Lumikki heard him open the refrigerator door.

Now. Stepping out from behind the door, she took two steps to build up speed and then silently slid in her socks across the almost unnaturally smooth hardwood floor to the stairs. Then she hurried up as quietly as the lion stalking that herd of wildebeest. She stepped into Elisa's room so inconspicuously that she succeeded in startling the trio waiting inside.

'God, you almost gave me a heart attack,' Elisa whispered. 'Now get in the closet.'

'Why?'

Lumikki didn't understand Elisa's train of thought. Tuukka and Kasper were happily sprawled on the couch clearly without any intention of hiding.

Heavy steps approached up the stairs.

'I'll explain later,' Elisa hissed, pushing Lumikki into the walk-in closet and quickly shutting the door.

'Is somebody over?' Elisa's dad asked from the top of the stairs.

'Yeah. Tuukka and Kasper came to keep me company,' Elisa answered in an affectedly cheery voice anyone could hear was an act from a mile away.

'Weren't you supposed to have a migraine?' he asked suspiciously. 'And aren't you boys supposed to be in school?'

'Oh, it just went away,' Elisa said.

'Maths class was cancelled because the teacher's sick,' Tuukka answered at once.

Lumikki watched through a crack in the door as Elisa's dad looked over the threesome. He had short blond hair and an upper body that suggested time spent in the weight room. The closet was dark but roomy. It smelled of girl. Lumikki's closet never could have smelled like that.

She was hiding again. Trying not to be seen.

Lumikki closed her eyes.

You can't run. We'll always find you. And when we find you, we're gonna kill you.

Kill.

You.

14

Du ska inte tro det blir sommar,
ifall inte nån sätter fart
på sommarn och gör lite somrigt,
då kommer blommorna snart.
Jag gör så att blommorna blommar,
jag gör hela kohagen grön,
och nu så har sommaren kommit,
för jag har just tagit bort snön.
Jag gör mycket vatten i bäcken,
så där så det hoppar och far.

A midsummer pole. Balloons, balloons, and more balloons, some escaping into the blue sky. The most beautiful evening of the year in the Åland Islands, already turning to night but still as bright as day. All of Dad's family there. The scents of summer, the distant screeching of gulls, the twittering of the swallows. Lumikki wearing a white dress and a garland of dandelions Mother made. She was singing Astrid Lindgren's 'Ida's Summer Song'. She didn't have a beautiful voice, and she wasn't used to speaking Swedish in front of people, but that didn't matter.

Cousin Emma, one year older, suddenly stood before her. Lumikki tried to get past. She wanted to go and see the midsummer pole. She wanted a balloon too, the ones Uncle Erik was filling with helium and passing out to the kids. A red one. Or blue. Not yellow under any circumstances. Perhaps red would be best.

'Want to play?' Cousin Emma asked in Swedish. Lumikki shrugged.

'How about we play that you're my slave and you have to do everything I say?'

Lumikki shook her head.

'Well, then I could be the queen and you could be my horse.'

'No,' Lumikki said.

'You have to. I get to choose because we live here and I'm older.'

Lumikki started to cry.

'No,' she said again.

Just then Aunty Anna, Cousin Emma's mother, came up with Lumikki's mum.

'Lumikki doesn't want to play with me. She just says no to everything I suggest,' Emma whined to her mother. 'She isn't even close to as fun as . . .'

'Shh . . .' Aunty Anna stroked Emma's blonde hair. 'Maybe Lumikki is a little shy,' she suggested. 'Come on, let's go get you a balloon.'

Aunty Anna took Emma by the hand. After a few steps, Emma turned back and stuck her tongue out at Lumikki. Aunty Anna and Mum didn't notice. Mum was looking out at the sea. It looked as though the salty wind was making her eyes water.

Wiping them with the back of her hand, she sighed and in Finnish said to Lumikki, 'It isn't always good to just say no. If you say yes a little more often, you could make some friends.'

Friends? Did Lumikki want friends? Did that mean she had to agree to do whatever people wanted?

'*Jag gör himlen vacker om kvällen, för jag gör den alldeles skär.*' The next line of the song didn't want to come out of Lumikki's mouth.

'No.'

Lumikki tried to say it in a voice that precluded any further discussion on the topic.

Elisa looked at her wide-eyed. That Bambi-just-lost-his-mother look didn't work on Lumikki.

'But none of the rest of us can,' Tuukka tried to argue. 'You're the only one Elisa's dad has never seen before.'

'Playing detective might have been fun in elementary school, but this isn't a game.'

Lumikki opened the balcony door and let the frigid air spill into Elisa's room. She had been forced to spend nearly half an hour in the saccharine smell of the closet while Elisa and the boys enjoyed themselves downstairs eating the chicken soup her dad had made. Finally Elisa's father had gone back to work.

Lumikki drew fresh air into her lungs. It didn't matter that it stung.

'But it might be the only way we'll ever find out what's going on,' Kasper said, joining in the coaxing.

'Or maybe we should stop this fooling around and go talk to the police,' Lumikki said.

No, no, no. Because of the party. Because of the drugs. Because of the break-in at the school. Because of the money. Because Elisa's dad was a cop and who was going to believe them unless they had more information, more than a few pictures and a deleted email?

'Ditching school day after day might not matter to you guys, but I'm not interested in flunking out.'

Determined, Lumikki set off downstairs. Elisa, Tuukka and Kasper followed her like puppies. All that was missing were the lolling tongues.

'All you have tomorrow is two hours of physics and two hours of PE,' Elisa said. 'And you're not anywhere close to missing too many classes in either of them.'

Lumikki glanced at Elisa. Had she checked on her class schedule and absences? Pretty smart move. Surprisingly smart.

'If you do this one more thing, I swear I won't bother you any more.' Elisa looked sincere.

Lumikki didn't give any sign that she was tempted, either by the idea that they wouldn't bother her any more or the actual task. She knew she would be good at it. She was good at being invisible.

'Okay. But now I'm going to school. I can still make art class.'

Elisa's expression brightened when she realised Lumikki had actually agreed. Spontaneously she hugged Lumikki, who felt as if a boa constrictor had her in its coils. She should have rebuffed Elisa's first surprise attack. Now she was clearly trapped in a downward spiral of hugging she was never going to escape.

'Thank you thank you thank you.'

Lumikki wriggled out of the embrace.

'Don't make me change my mind now.'

Tuukka was standing above them on the stairs, leaning on the railing and smiling crookedly. He probably thought his slanted smile was ironically sexy, but really it just looked stupid.

Outside, Lumikki looked at the clock on her phone. It was 12:35. She would have to be back here in seventeen hours.

The attacker came at Lumikki from the right. Quickly she delivered two right jabs to his nose followed by two uppercuts to the chin. Immediately she repeated the sequence. Two jabs, two uppercuts. Jab, jab, up, up. Lumikki's pulse was pounding around 175.

Her opponent staggered but stayed upright and continued trying to get a hold of her. Lumikki aimed her right elbow at his rib cage and then lifted up lightning fast, continuing the motion with her right fist directly into his cheek. Then she finished the job by lashing out with a quick side kick.

Her attacker lay on the ground. Sweat streamed down Lumikki's back, calves and face.

Her attacker attempted to rise, but Lumikki pushed him back firmly to the floor with her right hand.

Don't try anything, you little shit.

She started hitting with her right hand, letting her fist fall with all her force on her opponent's upper body and face. At first the blows were slow, accurate and inexorable. Little by little their speed accelerated and they turned wild, an angry flurry of hate.

Useless to beg for mercy. This isn't your parish church and you're not going to be pardoned for your sins.

Salty sweat ran into Lumikki's eyes, making them sting. She tried to blink the sweat away, but finally she had to squeeze her eyes shut tight. She didn't need to see. She knew her opponent's face all too well.

'With my fist in your face, and your face on the floor.'

You're. Never. Getting. Up. Again.

'Excellent! Now the same on the left side. You already know this combination. Go all out right from the start.'

Lumikki took a couple of extra sidesteps to her towel and used it to quickly dry her eyes and forehead. Then the pounding music again filled the gym where about forty young women, a couple of middle-aged women and three men began moving through the same synchronised pattern of steps and strikes like the parts of a finely tuned machine. This was Combat class.

Lumikki checked in the large mirrors on the walls that she was crouched low enough and her block was up high enough in front of her face, which was red from exertion. Diagonally behind her a girl in a green shirt and pigtails glanced at Lumikki to copy her form. *Go right ahead and look.* Lumikki knew she was one of the best in the group. She did every movement flat out and followed through. She had the technique down.

The choreography. Because in the end that's all this was. A series of movements performed in time to bouncy pop songs with a dash of martial arts thrown in. Simple enough steps for anyone to follow as they sweated their cellulite away fighting imaginary opponents while the instructor yelled directions and encouragement. Only a couple of degrees more aggressive than aerobics.

Lumikki liked Combat anyway. You worked up a sweat,

your muscles got pumped, and getting into the right frame of mind was easy for her. She didn't even want to practise a real martial art or boxing. She knew perfectly well how sinking a fist into another person's stomach felt. She knew how blood erupted from a nose and how strangely warm it felt on the skin. Like half-cooled jelly or jam. She didn't want a real, living target for her attacks. She still remembered all too well what hitting a real person felt like, even though more than two years had already passed. The blue Nordic dusk of that afternoon in the schoolyard was burned into her memory. When it crossed her mind, she tasted bile in her mouth and smelled the sweet scent of perfume in her nose. The fragrance contained roses, vanilla, and a hint of sandalwood.

The song had changed, but the pace remained frenetic.

'Let it rain over me, I'm rising so high, out of my mind, so let it rain over me.'

Lumikki didn't need rain to drench her black tank top. It was soaked through with perspiration as it was.

After class she sat in the dressing room, allowing her breathing to level off as she unwound the wraps from her hands. In addition to supporting her wrists, they also absorbed sweat. But more than anything they were part of the game, props for a role, a way for good little schoolgirls like her to imagine they were something else. Attitude wraps, some people called them, some in amusement, some more enthusiastically.

'This new programme is good. More intense than the old one.'

Lumikki glanced towards the person addressing her. The girl, who looked a couple of years older than her, was sitting at the other end of the bench, unwrapping her own wrists and clearly directing her words at Lumikki. Long red hair in a high ponytail. Face and arms dotted with freckles. Loose black trousers and a tight black top, the same Combat uniform Lumikki had on. She had seen the girl in class and around the gym lots of times. And she knew the girl had seen her too. Lumikki had noticed her watching her movements. And not just her movements but also the curve of her body, the shape of her muscles. She had sensed that the girl would talk to her at some point.

'Yeah, it's pretty good,' Lumikki replied.

With a relaxed, natural motion, the redhead slid over to sit next to Lumikki. Calvin Klein One and grapefruit-scented shower gel struggled for attention beneath the smell of her sweat. A tight bicep rounded as the girl continued removing her wrist wraps. Just at her bicep seven freckles almost formed the constellation Gemini.

Memories forced themselves on Lumikki. There was another person who wore CK One. Who had a tattoo of Gemini on his neck. How it had felt to press her lips to the skin of that neck and place feather-soft kisses along the stars. To let her mouth linger when it reached Castor. To know that somewhere around Pollux the owner of the tattoo would no longer be able to help turning, trapping Lumikki's wrists in his hands and kissing her on the lips.

Had that really been just the summer before? It could as easily have been a hundred years ago.

Lumikki grabbed her water bottle and took a long swig. The girl was clearly waiting for her to say something, to give some sign that moving closer had been a good idea. To take

121

a little initiative. Lumikki saw too well where it would lead. To more conversations, more smiles, a cautious invitation to coffee and then inexorably, inevitably to a situation in which she would have to be cruel.

It isn't you, it's me.

Not now. Not yet. Maybe not ever.

Let's just be friends.

And both of them would know that would mean doing their best to avoid each other from that point on.

And Lumikki would never be able to explain that they were in that situation only because the girl's perfume had reminded Lumikki of someone else. That was why they couldn't go on. She couldn't be honest. She would have to lie from the outset, and that would only lead to embarrassment, half-hearted regret, blunted vexation.

So pointless. Lumikki decided to save them both that time, to save the girl's feelings, and just continued drinking. The silence crossed the line into awkwardness. The girl shifted uncomfortably and brushed some stray hairs back

'Okay. See you later,' she said.

Lumikki raised one hand slightly in farewell. Grabbing her gym bag, the girl moved to another spot in the dressing room so they couldn't see each other. Lumikki quietly released the air from her lungs. That good, euphoric feeling she got after Combat was gone. Her skimpy workout clothes were plastered cold against her skin.

'I surrender. I surrender.' The last song from the session was stuck in her head, its repetitive refrain losing its motivational quality without the techno beat. In some things she preferred to

surrender than to fight. Sometimes that was better for everyone.

For once, Lumikki had the sauna to herself. Instead of throwing any water on the rocks at first, she let the warmth return to her skin, beads of sweat forming again, running from her neck down along her spine. Memories from the summer and autumn struggled to the surface along with the perspiration, although she tried to tell them this wasn't a good time. There was never a good time for regret and longing. Latching on to her, they clenched her stomach tight and forced her back to bend.

Light blue eyes looking straight into her own. Then quickly away. Somewhere away.

'It's better if we don't see each other any more.'

'Any more ever?'

'At least for a little while. You get that I want to work through this alone, right? I just can't be with you right now. And it wouldn't be fair to you to make you put up with me.'

Lumikki had wanted to scream. What right did anyone else have to say what the limits of her endurance were or decide what was fair to her or not? Lumikki knew how to take care of herself. What had infuriated her was how casually she had been shut out of this other person's life and challenges. As if she was a little, delicate child who needed protecting. Lumikki had felt like hissing back that she had been through much worse and didn't need to be kept in bubble wrap.

She had realised that shouting wasn't going to help anything though. She had made her decision. Lumikki's role was just to accept it. That was what the script said she did in this scene.

'What does "a little while" mean? I can still call you, right?'

Lumikki had detested the high-pitched pleading in her voice.

She had felt a lump of uncried tears growing in her throat and knew she would not know how to get it out. Years had passed since she lost the ability to cry. Last summer she believed she would be able to find it again, but during that conversation she had understood that she would just have to live with that lump, to swallow it and hope it would disappear on its own at some point.

No calls, no emails, no Facebook messages, no letters, no Morse code with a flashlight during the dark hours of the night, no smoke signals blown with steaming breath on a chilly autumn night, no burning thoughts so intense that they could penetrate fog and walls and doors. Nothing. Complete silence. It was as if the whole person had disappeared from the face of the earth. At least they had disappeared from Lumikki's life in one swift stroke. Just as unexpectedly and presumptuously as they had come.

Lumikki remembered that day in May. The startlingly bright sunshine and the temperature stealing like a thief past twenty degrees Celsius for the first time all spring. She was walking downtown with too many clothes on. On the shore by the rapids she took off her jacket and sat down on a bench to watch the dark water flowing by and feel the warmth of the sun on her face. It occurred to her that the moment would be perfect if she was eating her first ice-cream cone of the summer. Fortunately an ice-cream stand was right there next to her. Lumikki swung her jacket over her shoulder and went to the stand to bring up the end of the long line. Plenty of other people were craving their first cold treat of the summer too.

As she waited in line, Lumikki wondered whether she should

get liquorice or lemon. Liquorice was her default choice. And it was good. But the lemon was also interesting. Maybe it was the May light and the sun promising a long summer of stifling heat. When her turn came, she still didn't have her mind made up.

The light blue eyes of the boy behind the stand measured Lumikki as she opened her mouth to make her order. The boy was faster though.

'Don't say anything. Let me guess. You don't want chocolate or strawberry. And definitely not vanilla. You aren't interested in that caramel fudge stuff or any of the new flavours that you mostly think are just a way to trick the stupid and the curious. You're a liquorice girl. It's obvious a mile away.'

The light blue eyes narrowed a touch and then refocused.

'But right now what you want is lemon. Because it isn't really spring any more but it also isn't quite summer yet. You want something sour and yellow. May sun ice cream.'

Lumikki was speechless.

'You'll have one scoop, but you don't want a waffle cone because you think they taste like mildly sweetened cardboard. So I'll put it in a little cup.'

The ice-cream boy turned to fill the order. Suddenly Lumikki was unbearably hot. She would have been hot even if she had stripped down to her underwear right then and there. He took so long. The awkward moment stretched out. Lumikki still hadn't been able to say anything. Finally the boy turned and handed Lumikki a paper napkin and a bowl of ice cream. When Lumikki started digging in her pocket for money, a smile flashed in the light blue eyes.

'Don't worry about it. My treat.'

Lumikki managed to splutter something resembling a thank you and then turned on her heels with burning cheeks. She felt as if she had just been X-rayed. The feeling was extremely uncomfortable and also strangely tingly. When she returned to her bench by the rapids, she noticed something written on the napkin.

'Call. You know you want to.' And a phone number.

Lumikki shook her head to herself. *Presumptuous*, she thought. *And probably a jerk.* That night she dialled the number with sweaty hands.

Selfish jerk. Pathetic coward. Good-for-nothing quitter. No matter how many times Lumikki repeated those words through the slow, endless hours lying awake at night after their break-up, they never turned true. She had loved a jerk, a coward, a quitter. She had understood his decision even though she didn't want to understand. She had waited and hoped, hoped and waited, jumping every time the telephone rang, sitting at her window looking down on the street imagining she saw that familiar gait. She made strong black coffee in the middle of the night since she knew she wouldn't be able to sleep anyway. The pungent smell of the coffee was comforting, wrapping around her like a warm blanket. Intentionally she drank the coffee too hot, trying to dissolve the lump in her throat.

Over weeks and months the lump shrank and the longing took a step into the background. She wilfully gave up on hope. It wasn't any use. They would probably never meet again.

Lumikki began throwing water on the rocks, continuing until the stove stopped answering with an angry hiss. Hot steam painfully struck her upper back and neck. Lumikki straightened her back and felt the clenching in her stomach relent. Her eyes stinging, she wiped them with her hand. It was sweat, only sweat.

That evening Lumikki stared at the white wall of her apartment and thought about the painting she was working on in art class. She wasn't a particularly gifted painter or illustrator, although she did love the visual arts. She didn't hold out any hope of ever becoming more than a middling amateur. She took art classes just for fun, enjoying the chance to play and relax by making pictures. She doubted she would have access later in life to the free paints, canvases and studio the school offered.

Black, black, black. The surface had already been covered, but Lumikki had wanted even more black, more texture, cracks and crevices so the painting wouldn't just be two-dimensional. Once she had enough layers, she laid the canvas out on the studio floor on newspaper and, climbing onto a chair, began dripping red paint onto it. The drops of paint splashed against the black like red drops of rain, like drops of blood.

Lumikki had almost finished it today.

And now she knew the painting's title too. *Girlfriends*.

THURSDAY, 3 MARCH

15

White, tufted, puffy, gauzy, like mountains of whipped cream. Far off and further off, rolling over and past and under each other. Slowly, languidly moving clouds.

'*Day cools towards evening time . . .*' The words of a Swedish poem ran through her mind.

The day hadn't cooled yet. The peak of the heat was just passing. The air was like nectar. As if stroking the contours of her body with a great feather, it caressed toes, thighs, and arms. Out on the dock they could lie completely naked looking at the sky and the clouds. Waiting. Yearning. Longing for the other while only separated by a matter of steps. Smiling to herself, feeling that look on her skin.

'*Take my slender, longing shoulders in your hands . . .*'

Warmth from the air and from within. Warmth that dispelled idle thoughts. Hastening leisure, languid haste. The endless, endless transience of summer. The moment when everything was still good and being together was better than being alone. The thought that this feeling could last and last. *We could just stay here. I could be with this person. I could take that hand dozens, hundreds, thousands of times. And be quiet. Be quiet and hear*

*our breath seek the same unforced, tranquil rhythm that could
also accelerate together, in harmony.*

When summer had passed and a cold undertone appeared in
the wind as it scattered the first yellow leaves from the birch
trees, those thoughts felt like a dream. Like a dream someone
else had dreamed.

Lumikki sighed and moved her gaze from the sky towards
the police station. The large windows of the bus depot offered
an unobstructed view of it. This was her third hour of waiting
for something to happen.

This was senseless.

She had followed Elisa's dad, Terho Väisänen, from their home
in Pyynikki through the bone-chilling cold to the highway. Then
Väisänen had turned and gone to work and Lumikki had taken up
her watch in the bus depot. She wasn't about to go and wait at the
police station itself. Although the passport processing lines were
famous for how slowly they moved, a girl sitting in the waiting
room for hours on end would have aroused suspicion at some point.

Now no one was glowering at her. She was well groomed
enough that she didn't look homeless and inconspicuous enough
that no one would even remember her being here later.

Still, spending her day like this felt ludicrous. The most likely
scenario was that Väisänen would stay at work until four or
later and then walk home the same route he had come. Quite
the madcap stakeout.

Lumikki was on her fourth paper cup of black coffee. She
had to stay awake somehow.

Money. Men chasing Elisa. The young woman in the
photographs. Polar Bear.

How did all these things connect?

Väisänen was the key. She was sure of that. Elisa was sure too, even though she didn't want to believe anything bad about her dad. But she had to. After seeing the pictures, her face went somehow grey. Something inside her collapsed. In that moment, what remained of the innocence of her youth disappeared and a part of her identity shattered.

Lumikki recognised the feeling. She remembered looking at herself in the mirror sometime in the autumn of first grade, a little before Christmas, and seeing a frightened, shocked little girl who never could have believed that something like that could happen to her. That anything like that even existed. *I am no longer me.* That was what she thought. And it was true. She had become something else, a different kind of girl.

Once upon a time there was a girl who learned to fear.

Weary from watching the police station, Lumikki rested her eyes by looking around the bus depot for a while. Renovated about a year earlier, it was a beautiful functionalist-style building. The morning light rippled in through large windows. If you only looked at the light and not at the dazzling brightness outside, you could imagine it was summer.

Lumikki would have liked to lean back in her waiting hall chair, close her eyes, and dream once more of warmth and abandon. To accept the joy and sorrow of those memories. What the hell was she doing here?

Viivo Tamm kept one eye on the police station as he filled in his tabloid Sudoku. He was beginning to doubt Boris Sokolov's mental health. Lying in ambush all day for an on-duty police officer didn't feel all that smart. But Sokolov was sure that something funny was going on. He was puzzled by Väisänen's lack of response to Natalia's email. Apparently Natalia had giggled once about how Väisänen usually replied to her almost before she had clicked send.

Sokolov had this hunch something was going to happen today. When Sokolov had a hunch, there was no point arguing.

Viivo had asked Sokolov why he couldn't just go talk to Väisänen. To make him understand it wasn't a good idea to start screwing them around. Viivo was good at convincing people to stay in line. And to keep quiet. Some people never said anything ever again after he paid them a visit.

Apparently that wasn't an option this time. None of them could be seen with the cop if and when they wanted to continue their collaboration. So he was just supposed to watch.

Sokolov was convinced that Väisänen was playing his own game, and he wanted to know whether he had accomplices.

Did that square need a nine or a seven? Should have picked a three-star Sudoku instead of a five. Keep it simple. He wasn't trying to become a Sudoku master or anything, just kill some time. Biting the end of his pencil, Viivo glanced up at the police station.

This was going to waste his entire day.

Lumikki started digging out her phone to call Elisa and take back her promise. She had already wasted enough of her life on this futile stakeout.

Terho Väisänen thought about the email he had received late the night before. Of course he hadn't been able to contact

Polar Bear directly, but he did manage to get in touch with one of his 'assistants', who also used a code name. The assistant had emailed that Terho should visit the Tampere Convention Centre to retrieve a cell phone hidden in the tank of the third toilet stall in the men's restroom and use it to call the first number in the contact list. Then he would receive further instructions. The phone would only be there today.

Was he trying to bite off more than he could chew?

He could keep working with Boris Sokolov and the Estonians. They were straightforward mid-level criminals. Sokolov was a tad above the Estonians but still just as much an underling. Polar Bear was another thing. There were only rumours about him, no concrete information. Terho didn't know anyone who had actually seen him.

But if he wanted his money, he had to do something. And he really wanted it. He had to have it. He had been counting on it, and a couple of gaming debts were threatening to come due.

Pulling on his coat, Terho silenced his grumbling stomach and decided to spend his lunch hour in the convention centre's restroom.

A man walked out of the police station.

Viivo Tamm perked up.

Lumikki perked up.

Viivo was slightly faster, which was lucky for Lumikki, giving her just enough time to realise that the man who suddenly left his Sudoku looked familiar. When the man sprang into action, Lumikki recognised him from the length of his stride, his slightly hunched posture and the way he swung his arms.

One of her pursuers.

The man rushed out of the door. In the blink of an eye, Lumikki understood that the two of them weren't here at the same time and especially weren't charging out at the same moment by accident. One fact connected her and this man.

The same target.

Damn it. That was going to make everything more difficult. She would have to stay out of sight of two men.

16

Lumikki stood in the lobby of the Convention Centre, momentarily indecisive.

So far everything had gone well. Elisa's dad had been so focused on reaching his destination and his pursuer so focused on tailing him that neither had paid any attention to Lumikki. She had hung back as far as she could while maintaining a visual connection with both men. Now you see me, now you don't. She knew this game.

After crossing the railway bridge, they passed the university and turned north towards the convention centre. Inside she ran into a problem.

Terho Väisänen walked resolutely along the main concourse, following Kimmo Kaivanto's *Blue Line*, a stripe of tiles running down the middle of the floor that occasionally rose towards the ceiling in the form of blocky cobalt statues. Then Väisänen turned into the men's restroom. His pursuer paused for a few seconds outside, glancing around and then entering as well.

Lumikki considered her options. She could wait in the lobby, hidden from view. However, something decisive might happen in the restroom. Would probably happen in the restroom. No way had Elisa's dad come all this way just to get a little variety in the colour of tile he stared at while he peed. He had some other reason, and Lumikki had to find out what that was. She couldn't go inside as a girl because she would attract too much unwanted attention. So she would have to go in as a boy.

Lumikki looked at herself in the mirrors next to the cloakroom. She was wearing dark clothing and a grey skull cap. All appropriately gender neutral. A thick winter coat concealed the shape of her body. Quickly tucking her hair under her hat, she changed her posture, shifting her centre of gravity slightly. She altered the expression of her face.

The transformation was striking. In the mirror a teenage boy with his hat pulled down low glared back at her.

The gait was the most important thing. She had to relax, opening her hips and slouching slightly. Then she walked up to the men's room door, grabbed the handle and yanked it open confidently.

Terho Väisänen's fingers slipped when he tried to lift the lid of the toilet tank. It was surprisingly heavy and tight fitting. He tried to get his fingernails into the tiny gap, but it didn't help. He needed something longer. Terho rummaged in his pockets. His reflector armband wasn't going to be any help, nor was his driver's licence. Fortunately in the bottom of one coat pocket he found an old bike lock key, which he was able to wedge under the lid. Then he started wrenching the tank open as quietly as possible. Suddenly he heard someone enter the neighbouring stall.

Just his luck. Couldn't he ever catch a break?

138

The key was bending dangerously, but thankfully the lid was also shifting. It banged nastily against the edge of the tank. It sounded like an explosion in the quiet restroom.

The door opened again. Great, another set of ears. The newcomer chose the other adjacent stall. Terho felt surrounded. Now he just had to calm down, breathe deeply and try not to be paranoid. The convention centre was a public place with free toilets. Of course there would be other people here. It was just an unfortunate coincidence that three men wanted to empty their bowels at the same time. Well, two.

Terho removed his coat and rolled up his shirtsleeves. Shoving his hand into the water tank, he groped around. At first his fingers only felt water, and he was revolted despite knowing full well that the liquid was perfectly clean. Was he sure he was in the right stall? And what if they had already taken the phone back? Or what if he had been tricked?

Then his hand hit something.

Bingo.

Terho pulled out a black case, which was apparently waterproof. Opening it carefully, he found a cell phone wrapped in plastic. Shoving the phone in one coat pocket and the case in another, he replaced the toilet tank lid. His heart was pounding in his ears like an insane drummer. He realised his hands were shaking. Fear made his knees weak, even though there shouldn't have been anything to be afraid of.

Coat on, door open, quickly to the sinks. Vigorously rubbing soap into his hands, Terho washed and rinsed thoroughly and then repeated the process. He fought back his desire to go and wipe his fingerprints off the water tank. That would have been excessive.

Not a peep came from the other toilet stalls. *Maybe a little constipation going around*, Terho thought, drying his hands carefully and then hurrying out of the room.

Lumikki counted the seconds. With a quick glance down, she had made sure she entered a stall next to Väisänen. He had been struggling with something, based on the noises with the toilet tank. After finishing the job, he had washed his hands and left.

She heard the pursuer flush. For the sake of appearances presumably. Then he left the restroom too, without washing his hands. Lumikki detested it when people didn't wash their hands after using the bathroom. She wasn't a clean freak by any means, but that was just basic hygiene.

Five, six, seven, eight . . .

At ten seconds, Lumikki opened the stall door, washed her hands, and exited the lavatory. She just had time to see Terho Väisänen walk out of the building with the other man trailing. Lumikki had to hurry.

The park and duck pond outside looked enchanted. Every trunk and branch was either covered in thick rime or snow frozen in delicate crystalline formations. Sunlight reflected off every facet. Glittering, glimmering, glistening, sparkling, scintillating. The Snow Queen had ridden her sleigh through the park with hair and gown streaming, leaving behind infinitesimal ice crystals suspended in the air. She had made everything white and magical.

The breath of the Snow Queen. Ice and wind.

Lumikki's breath. Water vapour that quickly formed frost

on her scarf and the delicate, almost imperceptible hair of her cheeks.

Stopping at some exercise equipment along the jogging path, she did a few pull-ups, listening carefully. Terho Väisänen had just removed a phone from his pocket, fiddling with it for a few seconds and then walking towards the pond with it pressed to his ear.

His pursuer stood behind a nearby tree pretending to light a cigarette. Apparently Väisänen still hadn't noticed him. He had probably noticed Lumikki doing her pull-ups but wouldn't think some kid out for a jog would be interested in his telephone conversation. He also probably thought he was far enough away that no one could hear. However, in the perfectly still winter air, sound waves carried a long way.

Three, four, five.

Lumikki counted pull-ups as she waited for Elisa's dad to start his call.

'Hello? This is . . . Okay, you know who this is.'

The English made understanding harder. Väisänen spoke in a low voice facing the pond, which meant some of the words got lost along the way. Filling in the gaps would have been easier in Finnish.

Lumikki's arms began to tire. She obviously hadn't been doing enough pull-ups lately. She didn't give up though.

The pursuer was clearly listening too.

Twelve, thirteen.

'Polar Bear . . . So soon . . .? Eight o'clock tomorrow. Right. Black tie. If you could just . . .'

The last sentence was cut off. Someone had clearly hung

up on Terho Väisänen. Lumikki had heard enough though. So Elisa's dad was going to Polar Bear's party the next day after all.

Lumikki's arms failed her, sending her thudding to the ground, muscles trembling and sore from the exertion.

Crap. So much for staying invisible.

Väisänen and his pursuer both turned to look in her direction. There was no way she could continue following them. Now the most important thing was to suck it up and finish playing her role as the innocent athlete.

Lumikki started jogging around the duck pond, trying to maintain her masculine posture. Her combat boots slipped on the icy walking path, too obviously breaking the illusion. But they weren't going to turn into cleated winter running shoes simply by thinking about it. She just had to keep her chin up.

Nothing to see here, folks, just a kid out for a run.

If she could only get around the pond, she would have a straight shot home to a cup of something warm and an opportunity to make her report to Elisa.

Lumikki knew her hope was in vain when she heard heavy footfalls approaching from behind.

17

Boris Sokolov tried to call the Estonian, but he didn't pick up. He had probably switched his phone to silent in order to focus on the stakeout. That was smart enough, but the whole job was pointless now. Boris had just received a message from Polar Bear saying that Terho Väisänen had been in contact with him and that Polar Bear's men had delivered an invitation to the party by rather unorthodox means. Boris didn't always understand Polar Bear's methods. Sometimes he wondered whether Polar Bear was really so cautious or whether running people around was just the name of the game. The latter possibility felt just as plausible as the first. Sometimes following Polar Bear's orders could be exhausting. Boris knew he was in a privileged position, even a favourite of sorts, but that position could be taken away at any moment. He lived in constant fear, an invisible noose around his neck. He didn't have room for even a single mistake.

So it was best to stay focused on the job at hand. There was no reason to risk someone connecting the Estonian to their police informant. Or of Tamm going and doing something impetuous. Viivo Tamm was a good man, a professional, but occasionally he lost his cool. When that happened, he could become unpredictable and difficult to control.

Boris sent him a text message. It said: *Stop. Abort mission.*

Viivo Tamm sped up. This time the little bitch wasn't going to get away from him. This time he would show her. The first time had been a fluke. Now it was personal. His phone buzzed in his pocket. Someone was trying to call, but Viivo didn't have time to answer just now. He had business to attend to.

At first Viivo hadn't been able to place what was so familiar about the boy at the pull-up station. Then he looked closer. The coat. He had seen it somewhere before. When the boy started running, Tamm remembered. The boy wasn't a boy, he was a girl. A girl running a little differently somehow but similarly enough that he recognised her.

But why hadn't Väisänen recognised her? His own daughter?

Processing this took Tamm a few seconds, but when the insight came, it hit him like a ton of bricks. The girl wasn't the cop's daughter. This girl was someone else entirely who was somehow mixed up in all of this. And Viivo was going to find out how.

When the girl sped up, Viivo filled with rage. No teenage bitch was going to cross him. Because of her he had frozen his fingers and toes, using up precious dealing time skulking in the bushes in Pyynikki and filling in Sudoku puzzles in the bus depot. The girl in the red hat had made a fool of him.

He was going to catch her and squeeze her until she told him what her connection was.

She was going to learn not to play grown-up games when she didn't know the rules.

* * *

Up along a narrow path flanking the convention centre, uphill towards Kaleva Street and over it. Ice, slippery, completely the wrong shoes for running. Lung-rending cold and a bulky coat. Winter running clearly wasn't her sport.

Lumikki glanced back.

The man had nearly caught up with her.

Lumikki tried to breathe through a gap in her teeth. Hissing as she ran. *She sells sea-shells on the sea-shore*. The frigid air was merciless.

Across Kaleva Street to the other side.

Cold, cold, cold, cold. Cold hands, cold heart. Cold hands, cold heart. Words pounded in Lumikki's head as she tried to think rationally. Should she continue along Kaleva Street? Pluses: other people, cars. Minuses: patches of black ice and the possibility that the pursuer's accomplices could be lurking somewhere with their van ready to nab her at any second. Would they dare? In broad daylight?

Lumikki made a quick decision as she reached the next crossroads. The walking path was less icy there. Turning, she ran towards the graveyard.

The man followed. Fortunately he seemed to be having trouble with the slippery spots too.

Cold hands, cold heart . . .

Stop it.

Lumikki tried to get something else stuck in her head.

'Run baby run baby run baby run . . .'

Sheryl Crow came to the rescue. Lumikki's combat boots kept slipping. She swore to herself. From now on she would have to start wearing ice cleats and running shoes all the time.

Just in case someone started chasing her. Which seemed more than a little likely in light of recent events.

She turned into the cemetery. She passed Väinö Linna's grave on the right, Juice Leskinen's on the left. Dead writers and singers might be able to save her from boredom on long winters' nights, but they couldn't do anything for her now. Was she really going to die surrounded by graves? How ironic.

She could hear the steps growing closer all the time. Lumikki knew looking over her shoulder was not a good idea now. If she did, she would lose precious seconds. Could she run to the chapel? Or to the crematorium pick-up door? Would someone be there? Could she get inside?

No running in the cemetery.

Her mother's voice. Her mother's rules. *Sorry, Mum. Not even you can know or control everything. Sometimes you just have to run.*

The dead don't care. The dead are dead. Corpses don't care even if the girl running over their graves is trying not to become a corpse herself. That was why she had to run, even though her feet slipped wildly with each step, even though the cold seemed to be filling her lungs with tiny puncture holes and sweat was streaming down her back under her heavy coat and sweater.

The tall spruces of the graveyard were frosted with white, rounding their lines. Their branches hung down under the weight of the snow, towards the headstones, towards any visitors.

The dead and the living. The living and the dead.
Come again to judge.

Lumikki could already hear the man's breathing. Not long until his hand would grab the back of her coat.

Then something happened. Lumikki heard a thud, a snarled cry and a string of curses in Estonian. She didn't understand them, but the intent was clear. She didn't turn, but hope lent her legs renewed strength.

Slipping and falling, Viivo Tamm banged his left knee painfully on the ice. Immediately he knew the game was up. He wasn't going to be running after the girl any more. He would be lucky to be able to limp back home.

Like a whipped dog.

Like a beat-down mongrel.

Again his rage boiled up inside. But now it was bigger, redder and more blinding. Propped on one knee, he drew his pistol.

He didn't think, he only felt with every fibre of his being that the girl had to be stopped. At any cost. He raised his weapon and aimed.

Lumikki heard a muffled crack. Then something whizzed past her thigh and struck a gravestone ahead of her, blasting a piece off.

A bullet.

The man was shooting at her.

Lumikki's pulse suddenly jumped twenty beats higher. Now she flew, no longer noticing the slippery ground or the cold air or the rivulets of sweat running down her spine.

Only after a long, long way did she dare to take a glance back. The man's silhouette was small but still visible on the central lane, holding his knee. Some friendly old lady had gone to help him.

There was no sign of the gun. No more bullets whizzed at her.

Lumikki continued running, which suddenly felt easy. She knew she had escaped.

This time.

Cracks ran through the paint on the ceiling, forming strange roads to nowhere. Lumikki lay on her bed, looking at the cracks crisscrossing and letting the anger in her grow. Against her stomach she clutched a worn-out, baby-blue stuffed rabbit that was missing an ear. The bunny accepted the hard, rough grip of her hands.

She had made it home, yanking off her combat boots and hurling her winter coat at the back of a chair. After stripping off her soaked sweater and the even wetter long-sleeved shirt underneath, she stood in the shower for half an hour, letting the water wash over her like heavy rain. She washed her hair with unscented shampoo and used fragrance-free soap. She always used odourless products. Not because she was allergic or overly sensitive to perfumes, but because she didn't want to smell like anything in particular.

Recognising a person from the shampoo, soap or lotion they used was all too easy, not to mention perfume or aftershave. Just a hint of a fruity soap could be enough to tell even a blocked-up nose that a certain person had just been in the same room. Most people couldn't identify other people's characteristic odours in public spaces – that took a more developed sense of smell – but anyone who didn't have the flu could pick out the cloying, pungent smells of perfumes.

Scents also triggered memories. The smell of pine resin shampoo brought back a summer night and dragonflies flitting over the surface of the water. Musky shower gel traced a sharp picture of wiry, muscular arms and a back with beautiful, prominent shoulder blades. It reminded her of the moments they lay embracing, laughing at some little thing no one else would think was funny at all. It made her think of the sharp, searching gaze of those light blue eyes before which she always felt bewildered and flushed. Her heart always skipped a beat and her legs went momentarily limp when someone walked past smelling of the same shower gel. Even though she knew before seeing that the smell did not surround the person she longed for. That's how strong the effect of smell is on memory.

A person might not remember how a stranger looked, but when you happened to smell his aftershave somewhere else, his burly frame, short hair, jeans and checked button-down shirt immediately appeared in your mind. For example, she might remember how this man walked and where. Whether he entered a certain door.

Lumikki didn't want that. She didn't want strangers remembering her. Or even necessarily all of her acquaintances. She wanted to be able to move about as invisible and as scentless as possible.

Lumikki had rinsed the fear and panic from her skin. She had treated the blisters on her feet from running in boots.

She had answered a call from her mum.

'Fine. No, school isn't too bad. Yes, I still have money.'

Lies. Well-intentioned lies.

When did she stop telling her mother everything? When she

started school? That was probably it. Or maybe even earlier, since in their family they didn't talk in general. Lumikki had never figured out everything they didn't talk about, but the lack of talking hung in every room so thick it hit you like cobwebs. Everyone minded their own business. The taboo topics could be completely bizarre, things an outsider would never guess in a million years. Such as, for example, the stuffed animal Lumikki was holding. Mum had brought it to her the last time she visited Tampere and said that it was Lumikki's favourite toy as a child. Looking at the bunny's jet-black eyes, Lumikki instantly remembered that it had really been someone else's favourite toy. Not hers, though she had played with it too. She had expressed the thought out loud.

'No, you must be remembering wrong,' Mum had said. 'This was your favourite toy and his name was Oscar.'

Lumikki had shaken her head.

'I gave him the name Oscar later. At first his name was Zany. Maybe I got him from a cousin or something.'

Mum didn't say anything to that, and Lumikki had taken that to mean that this was another of the many things they simply weren't going to talk about.

The cracks in the ceiling were like a star chart for a foreign sky. Flaws. She loved them. They were interesting. But now Lumikki was concentrating on anger, because it gave her power. She had been chased a second time, and now someone had shot at her. By rights she should want even less to do with any of this than before. But now she wanted to know, she wanted clarity, she wanted closure. And most of all she wanted these men to pay for their crimes. She didn't want to be afraid any more.

The fear would only end once all the cards were revealed.

That was why she knew what she intended to do the following day. Angrily hurling the bunny rabbit into the corner, she pulled out her phone and called Elisa.

With the aid of a cane, Viivo Tamm hobbled to his door and then struggled with the key. Holding the cane and turning the key while avoiding putting any weight on his left leg was difficult. Swaying off balance, he grimaced.

The excessively helpful old lady at the cemetery had practically forced him to call an ambulance and probably would have come along to make sure everything was all right if the paramedics hadn't assured her that Viivo was in the best possible hands.

After finding a hairline fracture in his X-ray, the ER doctor fitted him with a splint and sent him off with a cane and some strong painkillers.

Now he was finally home. Viivo couldn't remember his barren, dreary little studio apartment ever feeling so inviting. A cold beer, a couple of ibuprofens and maybe something else too. Mixed drug use at its best. Then he would call Sokolov, who had already left several angry messages on his voicemail.

Raving lunatic Russian. He felt like not returning his calls, but then Sokolov would have just come banging on his door.

A musty fug greeted Viivo in the entryway. At some point he really should clear away the mountain in the sink. But wait, there was also a strange hint of peppermint mixed in. As if someone had just eaten a cough drop in the apartment.

Closing the door, he limped into his combination

living-room-bedroom-office. He didn't have time to turn on the light, because someone did it for him.

Viivo did have time to register the meaning of the smell though.

Polar Bear's men.

The shot was only a muffled snap. Then Viivo fell on his back and blood welled out of his mouth like red paint.

FRIDAY, 4 MARCH

18

Skin as white as snow.

An enormous powder brush swept over Lumikki's face. She was pale after the winter but they weren't trying to hide it. Quite the opposite. The foundation cream was a step lighter than her natural skin tone. As was the powder. The transitions were hidden carefully under the arc of her jaw. The make-up equalised the colour of her skin and concealed the small blemishes, making her face unnaturally smooth. She looked like a porcelain doll.

Lips as red as blood.

Elisa carefully traced the outline of Lumikki's lips. The liner pencil ran along her cupid's bow, then the left side of her upper lip and then the right. Then came the lower lip with one sure stroke. Fading the lines towards the middle of the lips. That enhanced the impression of depth.

One layer of lipstick. Excess carefully removed with a paper towel. Then another layer. And finally red lip gloss in the middle of the lips to create an optical illusion of plumpness.

Hair as black as ebony.

Elisa arranged Lumikki's fringe and then sprayed it with a

fine mist of hairspray. Fluffing the rest of her bob cut, Elisa let another layer of hairspray fix it in place.

The hair dye had taken well. Lumikki thought about how strange it had looked when she washed her hair after giving the dye time to set and rivulets of blue-black snaked onto the white tiles. The dye had formed beautiful, otherworldly patterns on the floor until the drain sucked the tinted water down the pipes. Lumikki had rinsed her hair until the water ran perfectly clear.

Even stranger had been when Elisa sat her down in a chair, wrapped an old sheet around her shoulders, and started trimming her hair. First to her shoulders and then up a little below her ears. Black locks pattered to the floor. Lumikki took a while to get used to the idea that they were coming from her head.

Black, wet strands of hair curling on the floor. Like question marks without the dot. The whole situation was a question mark. Lumikki longed for that missing dot, something to put a full stop to everything that had been happening. That was why she was here.

'You aren't regretting this, are you?' Elisa had asked in the middle of everything.

Lumikki almost smiled. 'Hair's just dead cells.'

Elisa shivered. 'I could never think like that.'

Lastly Elisa had cut her a fringe, straightened her hair and double-checked to make sure there weren't any strays poking out.

Elisa handed Lumikki a long, red evening gown whose colour varied from rose to orange and purple to burgundy as the fabric shifted and the light caught it in different ways. Lumikki put it on. The evening dress was simple, with thin straps and lines that draped perfectly on her form.

Lumikki lifted her eyes.

Mirror, mirror, on the wall . . .

The beautiful woman who looked back at her was a stranger with erect posture, mysterious dark eyes and an expression on her lips that could presage a smile or contempt. Lumikki was satisfied. This woman was not her. This woman was someone else. Someone who could get into Polar Bear's party.

Elisa bounced up and down making strange little sounds. Lumikki interpreted them as positive feedback.

'Oh my God, you're beautiful! I am so good. What the heck am I doing in high school when I could be the world's best make-up artist?'

Seeing Elisa happy felt good. The colour had returned to her cheeks and there wasn't that muzzy, forlorn emptiness lurking right behind her eyes.

'And now a little of this,' Elisa said and then spritzed Lumikki's neck with a perfume that Lumikki instantly recognised as Elisa's signature Joy.

Lumikki held her breath to avoid inhaling any of the mixture of essential oils and alcohol wafting in the air.

Now she smelled like someone other than herself as well. Good. No one would remember her from the party. What they would remember was a woman who looked like the Snow White from the fairy tales and smelled like expensive eau de parfum, hairspray and luxury soaps.

'Guys, come look!'

Tuukka and Kasper clattered in from the adjoining room.

'Well, were you able to get her . . . Wow!' Tuukka stopped mid-sentence when Lumikki turned round. Kasper's mouth literally hung open.

'Um . . . Wasn't it a different story where the dirty, mousy girl turns into a hot chick?' Kasper finally said. '*Cinderella*?'

'I'd hit that,' Tuukka said. He clearly hadn't had time to think before the words tumbled out of his mouth.

'In your dreams,' Lumikki volleyed back, restraining herself.

It was 7:20 p.m. Three hours earlier Lumikki had come over to Elisa's house, where Tuukka and Kasper had already gathered. The beginning of their meeting had been taciturn. They all knew that they had crossed some sort of line now. So far everything had been light somehow, controllable, exciting but not too exciting. Not any more. Someone had shot at Lumikki, and now she was going to a place where her life could truly be in danger.

Lumikki had told them her plan.

It wasn't sensible. It wasn't rational. It was dangerous. Lumikki didn't care. She wanted to be in danger now. She wanted to move towards what frightened her most.

When Lumikki got to the place in her plan where she would try to get into the party secretly through the back, Kasper opened his mouth and said, 'You won't be able to.'

'How do you know?' Elisa asked.

'You don't just "sneak in through the back" to get at Polar Bear. From what I've heard, they're going to have serious security there. Fences and guards and cameras and all that shit.'

158

Kasper clasped his hands behind his neck and leaned back in his chair. Evidently he was enjoying his role as the fountain of all knowledge.

'Okay. Then we can forget the whole plan,' Lumikki said.

Kasper smiled craftily. 'Except that you can walk right through the front door with everyone watching.'

'And how is that going to work?'

'Because women can. At least the kind of young women they invite to the parties to keep the men company and look pretty. Just so long as you're dressed for the theme, no one is going to ask you anything. And this time the theme is fairy tales.'

Tuukka spat sparkling water out of his nose. 'Are you serious? Do you really think we can make our little eco-anarchist lesbo look like some kind of high-class who— sorry, I mean . . . escort?'

Appraisingly, Elisa looked Lumikki over from head to toe. Then she announced that the boys could go and entertain themselves for a couple of hours watching movies or playing video games.

'I'll bet there are some things I can do that you two boneheads can't,' she said with a smile. 'And if Dad comes home, you keep him out of my room and say I'm sleeping or doing naked yoga or something.'

Lumikki was ready. It was 7:45. She had on her red evening dress and white high heels. She had practised in them for a few minutes until she'd learned how to balance her weight between her legs and how to walk, which was completely different from walking in low-heeled shoes. When all was said and done, it wasn't that hard. This was just another role for her to play, adjusting her own movements to match those of the image created by the clothes.

Lumikki doesn't know how to walk normally. She always shuffles around. She's so weird.

Words from ten years before. Lumikki remembered precisely the tone of voice in which they had been delivered. The expressions and gestures that emphasised the words. The exaggerated mimicry.

In that moment she had decided to learn to walk every possible way. Normally and abnormally, beautifully and unattractively, quickly and slowly, sauntering and mincing. So that no one would ever get to say anything like that to her again. It hadn't saved her then, but this skill had served her many times since.

Elisa helped Lumikki put on a short imitation-fur coat and then handed her long black gloves that reached to her elbows. Then, finally, a small beaded handbag.

'Don't lose that. It's crazy expensive,' Elisa said.

From downstairs they heard banging around as Elisa's dad prepared for the party as well. Tuukka and Kasper had gone downstairs too, preparing to go out. Lumikki snapped the handbag open. Inside were powder, blood-red lipstick in a gold tube, €100, and something fluffy and pink. Grabbing the fluffy surface, Lumikki felt her fingers sink in and then meet something hard. She lifted the object out of the handbag. Pink handcuffs.

Elisa shook her head, blushing. 'Don't ask. I don't want to remember that party.'

Lumikki raised her eyebrows only a fraction and then put

the handcuffs back in the bag. What Elisa did at her parties and with whom was none of Lumikki's business.

'And then this.'

Elisa handed Lumikki a long, black, hooded parka that reached almost to her ankles.

'I don't know what I was thinking when I bought this. I look like I'm wearing a sleeping bag when I put it on. But now we have a use for it.'

Lumikki put the parka on. Since it had to fit the fur coat underneath, it was a little tight in the sleeves, but otherwise it was perfect. Fastening the poppers, she carefully pulled the hood over her hair and looked at herself one last time in the mirror.

The Abominable Snowman's black cousin, I presume.

Elisa and Lumikki stood facing one another for a few seconds. Neither had any words. Lumikki wanted to hug Elisa and tell her everything was going to work out fine. Even though she wasn't at all sure of that. And she had never wanted to hug anyone voluntarily, except maybe her mum and dad when she was little.

Elisa was afraid. So was Lumikki.

Elisa was ready to do her part. So was Lumikki.

Asking Elisa whether she was really sure she wanted to dig any deeper into her father's business was pointless now. The time for questioning and hesitation had passed. Elisa might be a spoiled teenager who thought she was living the dream of a high-school debutante. Maybe she used to think she could skip through life buying designer clothes and handbags with her daddy's money, throwing out-of-control parties that someone

161

else would clean up afterwards, and throwing back drinks and a little more on the side, toying with boys and men alike at will. By burying her frailty behind a make-up mask. By pretending to be dumber than she was.

But Lumikki saw that Elisa knew this night was going to change everything. That it would shatter her rose-tinted fantasies once and for all. The first cracks had formed on Sunday night when Elisa removed her hands from that plastic bag and wondered why they were so sticky. But what would be revealed on this night could never be washed away by water and soap.

A moment of determination flashed in Elisa's eyes, making Lumikki wonder whether they were really so different after all. Their worlds were never going to match up entirely, but in fleeting moments like these they shared the same space, feelings and thoughts.

Elisa filled her lungs and then exhaled calmly.

'Now I'm going to go hug my daddy goodbye,' she said.

Lumikki nodded. The clock said 7:52.

19

Terho Väisänen's fingers slipped on the smooth satin as he tried to adjust his bow tie. His hands wouldn't stop sweating, and he had to keep drying them with toilet paper.

It was already so late. He should have been outside waiting for the car to pick him up. Under no circumstances did he want to be late. The car wouldn't wait. The opportunity would pass, slipping through his fingers like this satin bow tie.

A black-tie occasion. When was the last time he had worn a tux? Sometime years ago at a party his wife's boss threw. He would never forget that five hours of uninterrupted pretentiousness from the welcoming toast to the moment their taxi picked them up. He didn't like this kind of upper-crust soirée. Although in many regards he was part of the 'upper crust' these days too.

Finally the bow tie cooperated. Fidgeting, he combed his hair one more time, even though the barber had just arranged it perfectly. Terho realised he was more nervous than he had been in ages. He reminded himself he was going to the party for only two reasons.

To speak directly to Polar Bear and hopefully to see Natalia.

She still hadn't replied to any of his emails. Terho knew that she had been to Polar Bear's parties before, but she was never willing to tell him anything about them.

Top secret, my love.

Polar Bear's grip on people could be uncanny. Terho doubted he would have any kind of bargaining position in the man's eyes. After all, he was just a pathetic narcotics cop, a tiny player. Over the past ten years he may have done his own small part in helping Polar Bear's businesses, but he could probably have got along just fine without Terho too. Still, he had to try.

In the early hours of the previous morning, he had made a decision. He didn't want to go on. He wanted out of his double role. But in order for that to work, he needed some sort of compensation from Polar Bear to help patch the gaping hole that would be left in his future income. He had to be able to pay off his gambling debts and arrange things for Natalia and himself. Then he could focus on living an ordinary, peaceful life without anything to raise his heart rate. No crime, no gaming, no Natalia, no money.

He had realised that he couldn't handle the stress and fear any more. The secrecy that as a younger man had kept him high on an adrenaline buzz now just made him tired. He might be able to go on for a few more years, but then his health would give out. Maybe it would be his heart or maybe it would be his nerves, but either way he was headed for a crash. He had been deluding himself for far too long already.

Terho stared at the man in the mirror, who looked older than his years. The bags hanging under his eyes, the loose skin hanging under his jaw, the belly hanging over his belt.

Everything about him hung slack or overflowed. Years of stress and guilt ate at him, making him consume whatever passed in front of his mouth, neglect his health and well-being, neglect even his family. He had to admit that. If not to anyone else, at least to himself.

It had to end. Seeing Natalia also had to end. Given their shared past, they would never be able to appear in public together. He had to start a new, honest life. Which was why he was about to try something so reckless and unlikely to succeed. He intended to blackmail Polar Bear.

Terho glanced at his watch. Time to leave. He was just striding into the entryway when Elisa came tumbling down the stairs, grabbed his arm and started dragging him towards the basement.

'What now? I should already be gone,' Terho said irritably.

'I need to show you something really important. It'll only take a minute.'

'Not now. I can't be late. I have a really, really important event to attend.'

'How can some party be more important than me?'

Elisa kept a firm grip on her father's arm, looking at him with large, accusatory eyes. Now instead of his seventeen-year-old daughter, what Terho saw was the seven-year-old child he could never stand to disappoint.

'Okay. One minute.'

Quietly Lumikki slipped down the stairs, which was surprisingly difficult wearing high heels and the constricting sleeping-bag coat. Tuukka was waiting for her outside, hidden near the lower gate.

'Not here yet,' he whispered.

'Hopefully they aren't late,' Lumikki said. The temperature was a few degrees below freezing, a high for the winter.

A thin, white layer of frost covered every surface. Houses, trees, rocks, cars. Clothing, hair, cheeks, thoughts.

'Elisa promised to keep her dad busy until I call,' Tuukka said.

Then they were just quiet and waited. Lumikki wondered why Tuukka didn't make some lewd wisecrack about her black snowman costume or the propositions she was sure to get during the course of the evening. Then she noticed the tension in his jaw. Tuukka was nervous. Maybe even afraid. Probably for the first time in his life.

Once upon a time there was a boy who learned to fear.

Lumikki herself felt surprisingly calm. Now she was just following a set programme. All she had to do was concentrate on what would happen next.

At 7:58, a black Audi turned onto the street and stopped in front of the house. Tuukka looked at Lumikki, one eyebrow raised. She nodded. Tuukka started walking. Casually he passed the black car and then, once he was outside of the driver's field of vision, hid behind another vehicle parked further down the street and began moving back behind the black Audi, crouched out of sight. Then he stopped and waited.

Enter Kasper.

Starting from the corner, he moved towards the black car and then turned to walk in front of it. The driver did not react in any way. Removing a key from his pocket, Kasper showed it to the driver with an exaggerated flourish, pressed it with relish against the hood and continued walking, drawing the

166

key across the surface of the car. The screech of metal on metal cleaved through the otherwise quiet winter evening. At first the driver stared at Kasper as if not comprehending what was happening.

Then Kasper lifted his middle finger gleefully.

Finally the driver came to life. Bellowing something incomprehensible, he sprang from the car. With the driver distracted, Tuukka acted with lightning speed and opened the trunk of the car a crack. Kasper was already running away, laughing maddeningly as the driver charged after him, turning only momentarily to lock the car with his key remote and then continuing to chase Kasper, who was running just slow enough to remain temptingly close.

Lumikki was immediately at the car. Tuukka helped her into the trunk. Luckily it wasn't one of the smaller ones, but Lumikki still had to arrange her arms and feet carefully in order to fit. Finally she put a strip of silk fabric over the locking mechanism and gave Tuukka a thumbs-up to signal that everything was ready.

Tuukka replied with the same gesture and then closed the trunk as silently as possible.

When the darkness surrounded Lumikki, she had to fight against a moment of panic. She was in an uncomfortable, tight space that smelled like gasoline. She hoped the trip wouldn't take long.

Lumikki heard the driver return cursing to himself. Chirp chirp, and the locks opened. The driver climbed in and slammed the door shut.

Lumikki squirmed to see whether she could get her phone

out of her handbag. Just barely. She looked at the clock on the phone, which said 8:05. The brief blue glow from the display momentarily illuminating the darkness did her good.

Then she heard steps approaching from the direction of Elisa's house. A car door opened.

'What took you so long?' the driver asked irritably in English.

'Sorry. Family business,' Lumikki heard Terho Väisänen reply.

'Polar Bear hates it when people are late.'

'Let's not waste any more time then.'

Amen. Lumikki agreed completely with Elisa's father. She had no desire to spend any more time than was absolutely necessary in this place and position.

The Audi growled into life.

'You have criminals on this street.'

Lumikki could only just make out the driver's words, but they made her smile. When the car accelerated and cold currents of air began creeping through the gaps in the trunk, she grew serious.

There was no turning back.

20

The darkness was impenetrable. There was no way through it. It gave no ground.

She would never get out. She would never get air. She would die.

Gravel pressed a pattern of tiny depressions into her back. She squeezed gravel in her hands, feeling the sharp edges of the tiny rocks, letting them dribble between her fingers.

'Let me go!' she screamed.

She had already screamed it ten times, a hundred times, a thousand times. She had hammered on the lid with her fists, kicked it with her feet, turned over and tried to lever it open with her back. Nothing.

They were sitting on it. Probably dangling their feet and taking turns sucking a lollipop, savouring its strawberry flavour. They were in no rush. They had the power.

The tears had already dried in Lumikki's eyes. She was starting to panic. She felt like if she didn't get out right that instant she would suffocate.

She started to shriek. As loud as she could. She thought of the calls of seagulls and the way they opened their beaks so wide. She was a gull. She screamed.

The louder the sound, the more alive. She became the sound. She was one with the sound. The same red, raging, shrill note.

At some point she realised it wasn't dark any more. The lid of the gravel box was open. She sat up and wiped her tears. Grit stuck to her cheeks, finely ground gravel.

There was no sign of them.

They were waiting for their next opportunity. They knew just as well as Lumikki did that one would come.

Lumikki slowly counted to ten.

She couldn't panic now. She wasn't the same girl now as back then. She had changed. She had learned. She could stay in any small space for any length of time.

Everything had gone the way it was supposed to so far. Almost everything.

Yes, she had bruises from bumping against the sides of the trunk on some sharp turns. Yes, she felt as though she would be smelling the stench of gasoline for the rest of time. Yes, she was shivering with cold and numb from head to toe. But those were just little things.

The Audi had driven for thirty-five minutes, then slowed and finally stopped. Terho Väisänen exited the car first. Then the driver followed a moment later, locking the vehicle and leaving.

Lumikki had listened and then when everything around was quiet, she grabbed the silk strip with her stiff fingers and pulled evenly, pushing up on the trunk lid at the same time with her legs. She had to take the risk eventually. The fabric she'd jammed in the lock mechanism was supposed to shift the latch out of place so she could get out.

The sound of fabric ripping was the worst thing Lumikki had heard in a very long time.

Don't panic. Stay calm.

Lumikki felt with her fingers for where the fabric had ripped. She couldn't find it. Her fingers had lost almost all sensation and the long gloves she was wearing made feeling even more difficult. Lumikki grabbed her left glove with her teeth and pulled it off. Then she shoved her fingers in her mouth to warm them until the blood started flowing again.

Another attempt.

Her fingers fumbled around the area of the lock and felt fabric. Lumikki knew that her wet fingertips would freeze again in seconds.

Yes. Oh yes. Just enough silk remained that she could still get a grip on it. Clinging to the fabric, she pushed up powerfully with her legs and pulled the cloth slowly, slowly, slowly and steadily towards herself.

The lock didn't open.

Lumikki clenched her teeth, pushing and pulling. She strained with all her might.

Click.

The lock gave way. The trunk opened. Holding the lid open just a crack, Lumikki steadied her breathing. She listened. Just then another car pulled in next to hers and stopped. The people inside got out.

'You might think about vacuuming your car sometime,' a woman's voice said. 'Look at my shoes. They were supposed to be pink.'

'You're the one who wanted to be Sleeping Beauty. I think

171

the evil stepmother would have worked just as well. You could have worn black shoes then,' a man replied.

The quarrelling voices of the couple receded. Silence returned.

Lumikki lifted the lid a little more and peered out. She was in some sort of small parking lot. Fortunately the black Audi was right at the edge, in the shadows and a little behind some trees. No one was around just now.

With no time to spare, Lumikki peeled off her sleeping bag coat, pulled her glove back on, climbed out of the trunk, and quietly closed it again. She had to leave the parka. The driver would wonder about it the next day or whenever he next opened the trunk. Lumikki checked her hair with her hands. It felt like it was in miraculously good shape. Elisa hadn't exaggerated when she said the hairspray she used could work magic.

Powder compact out of handbag, mirror up. Quick check of make-up. Remove a little stray lipstick from one corner. Then she was ready.

Lumikki turned to look at the party venue.

Boris Sokolov inspected his creation and nodded to himself. The Snow Queen looked just like she should. If seeing this didn't make Terho Väisänen stop making trouble, Boris was willing to eat a gallon of ice cubes. In one sitting.

At once Boris felt an indefinable sorrow and satisfaction. The reason for the satisfaction was clear. He was relieved. He had worked things out with Polar Bear, and he wasn't angry about Viivo Tamm's shooting.

172

Polar Bear had argued that Viivo had been seen running amok with a gun in broad daylight in the cemetery. That just wasn't how things were done. It showed that the man had lost his touch, that he had started to slip. There was nothing they could do with a man who was slipping, of that Polar Bear and Boris were agreed.

So Viivo had had to be eliminated. It was nothing personal.

Sokolov looked at Natalia, whose brown eyes were open. Her face wore a confused, surprised expression.

Poor little Natalia – did you really think Big Bad Boris wouldn't find out about your escape plan? And then the money. That would have been stealing. And stealing, as we all know, is wrong. If you had just done what was right, everything would be different now.

Natalia, Natalia.

Snow Queen, frost on her lips.

The party could start.

Kasper's reports had been right. A tall stone wall surrounded the building, which itself was a large, three-storey house from the early 1900s that appeared to be located out in the middle of the woods. Only a narrow road led through the forest to the house.

Lumikki wondered whether the house was even on the map. There were places that certain people wanted to keep secret and there were ways to make that happen.

Lumikki started making her way towards the gate, where guards appeared to be stopping people and asking them something. Lumikki tried to look as much as possible like what she was playing. A high-class paid escort.

When Lumikki's turn came, she stepped past the guards, confidently yet slowly, in keeping with her station.

'*Hetkinen*. Stop,' one of the refrigerator-sized men said, repeating himself in Finnish and English.

Lumikki's heart jumped. Was this where it would end?

'*Kännykkä*. Cell phone,' the guard demanded, extending his hand.

Lumikki pursed her lips and then dug her phone out of her handbag, shoving it demonstratively into the man's enormous outstretched palm. Given her indignation, you would have thought this was a much more important object than Elisa's old cast-off phone. The guard slipped the phone into his bag, which, judging from the clatter, contained more than a few. Then, without asking her permission, he grabbed Lumikki's handbag, inspecting its contents and then giving it back with a grunt.

A barely noticeable movement of his head signalled to Lumikki that she could go through. She ordered her legs not to shake from the cold and relief. She kept her head up. Walking along the icy path in high heels was pure masochism, despite the gravel that had been carefully spread around.

One step at a time. Calmly.

Around her it was dark. Lumikki walked along a lane of light. The driveway was lined with luminaries whose flames flickered restlessly. At the end of the path was a door where the epitome of an old-fashioned butler stood. Slicked-back hair and short, white gloves. A language of gestures that simultaneously conveyed superiority and subservient civility. The man opened the door for Lumikki, bowing slightly. Lumikki stepped in.

She had succeeded.

She had really got into Polar Bear's party. Now she just had to find out what Elisa's dad was mixed up in.

21

Another world. Another reality.

Colours, lights, sounds. Blue that in an instant changed to green and yellow. Orange that turned to undulating gold. Violet that grew into sinuous garlands of burgundy, lilac and fuchsia. Music, the singing of mermaids, the sighing of forests, the tinkling of crystals, the forgotten echoes of deep caverns, the chamber orchestras of palaces and castles, the jingling of tiny bells, all sweeping over you, grabbing you from behind, disappearing and then returning again.

Wonderland.

Soundscapes and lights and props skilfully transformed each of the large rooms into its own reality. From a dark forest abuzz with secrets, Lumikki stepped into a silver ballroom with walls encircled by genuine rose garlands. She walked through an undersea kingdom. She peered into a log cabin with a small chair, a medium chair and a large chair.

The illusions entranced her so thoroughly that several seconds passed before she began to discern the details of the rooms properly. Waiters and waitresses bearing trays were everywhere. Of course, each room offered fantastical drinks appropriate to the theme. Some of them seemed to smoke and others shifted colour from purple at the bottom to light blue at the surface. Some of the staff were dressed as fairy-tale characters, some as gold-painted living statues.

Guests wandered from room to room with drinks in their hands. Amid the din of voices, Lumikki could pick out Finnish, English, Swedish and Russian at least. Somewhere she might have heard Spanish too, but she wasn't sure. Most of the women looked just like her. Young and dolled-up and like they didn't know any of the other attendees. Kasper had been right. A lot of these girls were being paid. The actual guests were mostly middle-aged men, a few older and a few younger. There was also the occasional couple. Lumikki recognised the slightly wizened-looking Sleeping Beauty and her prince. Both of them could have used some beauty sleep. If not a full hundred years, at least a few hours.

Some of the guests' faces appeared vaguely familiar to Lumikki. Were they politicians? Businessmen? Hard to say.

Lumikki tried quickly to visualise how the spaces connected. Evidently two floors were reserved for the party. The third storey had rooms for people to retire to 'rest' and the basement was for the staff. At least that was where the staff took their empty trays and then returned from with full ones.

'I don't imagine I could offer you one of these, could I?'

Lumikki turned to see a man holding two glasses. Apparently he had been directing his words at her. He was greying slightly, but most people would have called him handsome. His eyebrows were dark, his eyes brown, and his suit extremely well fitted. Out of the corner of her eye, she registered from the tag intentionally left on the cuff that it was Hugo Boss. So he wanted to pay a lot for his suit but was old-fashioned when it came to brands. It fit the image. In terms of his age, he could practically have been Lumikki's grandfather.

The man bowed to Lumikki. Lumikki restrained her desire to step back from the stench of cigars and aftershave. That was Hugo Boss too. Apparently the man wanted to triple underline the idea that he was a boss himself.

'Unfortunately it has apple in it,' the man said in a low voice, as if it were some great secret. 'I assume that's poisonous to you Snow Whites.'

A self-satisfied smile hovered on the man's suntanned face. He obviously thought he was extremely clever.

Lumikki searched her repertoire of facial expressions and chose a slightly stupid, flattered, flirtatious smile.

'Yeah. We're kind of allergic to it. But if you find me something else nice and strong and a little sweet, then we could talk some more.'

'Something strong and warming for a cold night like tonight,' the man said, setting his hand on Lumikki's bare arm in a caressing gesture.

His hand was clammy. Lumikki contained her shudder of disgust, restricting it to her thoughts.

'You read my mind.'

'Your wish is my command,' the man said. 'Don't go anywhere.'

'I'll try not to get lost in the woods. Or end up a house slave for seven undersized men.'

The man's smile widened.

'And if someone tries to dress you in a corset that's too tight, I promise to take it off,' he said, throwing her a wink.

Well now, the grey panther knew his Grimm. But familiarity with fairy tales wasn't going to score him any points with Lumikki. Or lead to any other kind of scoring. Lumikki watched as the man's broad back retreated. Then she slipped upstairs.

Terho Väisänen looked around. There was no sign of Natalia. His bow tie was uncomfortably tight around his neck. He loosened it.

Some of the guests made his eyebrows shoot up. *Is he really here? And him?* This material could have filled the pages of the national tabloids and a couple of gossip magazines to boot. He watched as a well-known politician nibbled the ear of an uncomfortable-looking Tinker Bell.

Terho knew that no one was going to breathe a word about the party to anyone. Polar Bear's men butchered snitches. And not just snitches but snitches' families, relatives, lovers and friends. Everyone knew it and no one wanted to be a cautionary tale.

He saw a young woman dressed as Snow White. There was something vaguely familiar about her. Didn't Elisa have a dress a lot like that? Well, apparently it was a popular style and not quite the one-of-a-kind the saleswoman had led them to believe. More evidence that you didn't always get what you wanted, even when you had money.

You could still get quite a bit with money though. You could get your life straightened out. And that was why he was here.

* * *

While the first-floor rooms were beautiful, enchanting fairy-tale worlds, those on the second were full of savage nightmares from the same stories. Trees whose limbs grabbed at passers-by like hands. Swamp sprites that used their songs to lure men into bottomless pools. Sleep that a prince's kiss could not break.

One room was black and contained an illusion of flying crows cawing threateningly. Instinctively Lumikki almost ducked to avoid the imaginary claws grabbing her hair.

Inside the room were two waiters dressed in black carrying silver platters. On the platters were small shot glasses full of black liquid. The waiters were talking to each other in hushed tones. Lumikki wanted to hear what they were saying, so she stepped closer, trying to look like she intended to take a drink.

'Where is Polar Bear?' one waiter asked.

'Haven't you heard he never comes until midnight?'

'He? I thought that . . .'

The waiter shot the other a warning look and extended his silver platter ever so slightly towards Lumikki. Lumikki took a shot glass, smiled and turned her back.

'Polar Bear has a strict rule that everyone always has to say "he",' the waiter whispered.

Lumikki tipped the glass so the liquid just touched her lips and considered what she had heard. She glanced at the large, ornate clock on the wall. Nine fifteen. Almost three hours left.

The other aspect of the exchange was a mystery. Why wouldn't they refer to Polar Bear as 'he'? Strange. Presumably that would be cleared up at midnight too.

Based on the party, Lumikki's picture of Polar Bear was becoming increasingly odd. He – or was he a he after all? – had used great sums of money to create all of these fantastic scenes for a single night. You could bet most of the guests were incapable of appreciating the lavish rooms. All that mattered to them was that the alcohol didn't run out and the girls were beautiful and open to flirtation. And maybe more.

Swine in black tie.

As if a €1,000 suit and a €20,000 watch gave you class. Or the right to act however you pleased. If you had money, there were no rules. If there were no rules, you were a king.

Suddenly Lumikki felt sick to her stomach. She wanted to go home. Instead of high heels, she wanted to pull on the grey slippers her grandmother had knitted her. She even wanted to fix herself a cup of tea, even though she usually thought it was nothing more than pointless warm stuff. Right now it would have felt calming and homely and reminded her of wallpaper with roses and her grandmother's gentle hands braiding her hair.

Lumikki carefully licked her lips. Liquorice vodka, just as she had guessed. The sharp, salty taste eased her nausea.

Remember, you aren't really here. This character is not you. Someone else is walking through these rooms in white high heels and a red evening gown. None of this can touch you.

Lumikki straightened her back. She wasn't here to have a good time. She had a job to do.

22

Natalia was not cold. She had been dead for 128 hours. One hundred and twenty-eight hours was a laughably short time when a person was alive. Dead, it was even shorter. Natalia had lived for twenty years, three months and two days. She would be dead for an eternity. Next to eternity, 128 hours was no time at all.

If Natalia had still been alive, would she have wanted to return to the moment when Boris Sokolov first contacted her? Natalia had met him a couple of times with her boyfriend at the time, a dealer named Dmitri, and knew that Sokolov was a big fish in the business. Not a high-level boss, but a boss nonetheless. He had influence. Sokolov invited Natalia to join his team. Apparently they needed a presentable-looking young woman with a brain unclouded by booze or drugs.

Would she have wanted to choose differently? If she hadn't said yes to Sokolov, she never would have come to Finland, she never would have met Terho Väisänen, she never would have tried to run away with the money, and she never would have taken that bullet in her gut. She wouldn't be lying dead now at minus eighteen degrees Celsius, eyes staring into the darkness, blue lips slightly parted as if ready to whisper something.

If Natalia had known what would happen, of course she would have declined. But all she had known back then was that she didn't want to raise her daughter in an apartment that stank of mould and whose cardboard-thin walls let through the neighbours' vociferous quarrels and equally boisterous make-up sessions. So she had agreed. That very same week, Sokolov arranged better living arrangements for Natalia, her mother and Olga.

A year passed. Natalia peddled drugs to the young, rich and affluent of Moscow, feeling that she was one of them. Young, rich and beautiful.

Life could have been good. Worth living. But in her nineteen years, Natalia had already learned that whenever everything seemed to be going right, something would always foul it up. That time it had been an order to leave for Finland with Sokolov to run the business there. She had imagined herself ending up in Helsinki, where flying home would be relatively easy. Instead she'd had to move to Tampere, which seemed pitifully small the instant she arrived. Before, Sokolov had spent half of his time in Moscow and half in Tampere, but now he moved to Finland full-time as well.

Orders from Polar Bear, Sokolov had said. That was the first mention Natalia had heard of Polar Bear. Later she had been invited to Polar Bear's parties and realised how ridiculously small her role in the grand scheme of things really was. She was a trivial cog, replaceable at a moment's notice.

Natalia felt as if she was on completely foreign ground in Tampere. She walked wrong and dressed wrong. Her rabbit-fur muff and high-heeled boots were over the top. People stared at her on the street. Men tried to offer her money but not for drugs, for sex. At times Natalia thought bitterly that the only way not to stand out from the locals was to wear a snowsuit in the winter and a tracksuit in the autumn and spring and spend the summer sitting on Tammela Square eating black sausage with a baseball cap on your head and knock-off Crocs on your feet.

She didn't know anyone in the city other than Sokolov and his Estonian sidekicks. In the beginning she called home every night, listening to little Olga's voice and then crying herself to sleep.

Sometimes she watched the Finnish high-school students, who looked like absolute babies in her eyes, even though she wasn't more than a year older than them. She wondered what it would feel like to live like them. To go to a coffee shop after school to debate the meaning of something a good-looking boy had said or what a teacher might ask in an upcoming history exam. To deliberate over future education options and consider taking a year off before college. To dream about moving out on your own, buying your own kettle and making your bed with those Finlayson sheets your grandparents gave you as a graduation present. To experience an existential crisis over not knowing what you wanted to do when you grew up.

Then Natalia had met Terho, who was completely different from Sokolov and the Estonians, even though Sokolov said he was 'one of us'. A narcotics detective who had got tangled up in the business, a mole.

Terho, and Terho's rough hands. Natalia had felt affection

for him from their very first meeting. He was so shy, so sweet and insecure about how to speak to her and how he could touch her. Completely different from her previous boyfriends and all the other men who immediately jammed her into the shape they wished, twisting her like a mannequin into the pose they wanted.

Had it been love? It had felt like love, at least. Natalia had felt safe with him. Terho talked about his home, his family, normal life. Natalia had known that she wanted a life like that too. Not this secrecy, this fear, the sensitive nasal membranes and needle marks in her groin. He had promised to arrange things for Natalia, to help her out. For a long time Natalia had believed him, but nothing ever happened. He had only been making empty promises, just like all the other men in Natalia's life.

Words that turned to lies the instant they left the mouth.

Natalia should have learned by now. Not to trust anyone but herself. To make her own decisions and bear the consequences.

That was why she decided to take the €30,000 meant for Terho from Sokolov's house and disappear. She made a plan. She stole Sokolov's spare key without him noticing. She arranged a hideout in the countryside. Everything should have been easy. On Sunday Sokolov and the Estonians were supposed to be away until the evening, but they came home early. That was why Natalia Smirnova was lying dead now, in the dark, naked.

She was bearing the consequences of her decisions, consequences that were heavier than she ever could have imagined.

Natalia's life had been a series of seemingly unavoidable

wrong decisions. Wrong decisions had been offered to her as right, presented on a golden platter smelling of roses. But she had never looked under the tray or past the person holding it to the white snow splattered with a shower of red droplets behind.

That was why Natalia Smirnova was lying alone now in the cold without feeling the chill.

Just as she had lain for the past 128 hours.

But even in death she could not be at peace. Boris Sokolov still had one more use for her.

23

Lumikki hurried down to the basement. Occasionally she glanced back to see if the man had followed her. No, thank goodness. She had managed to shake him off.

She had just been sampling the dozens of different delicacies at the buffet when the man who had accosted her earlier surprised her from behind and demanded an explanation for her disappearance.

'The ways of woman are inscrutable sometimes,' she answered coquettishly.

The man suggested that they move upstairs to investigate her feminine wiles a little more carefully. Lumikki begged him to let her eat first. In response, the man placed his hands on her hips and said that it would be a shame to ruin such a lovely, slender waist with excessive gluttony. Lumikki replied that she hadn't eaten all day and that he would probably prefer for her not to faint. The man laughed.

'You're probably quite the wildcat once you get going.'

Yeah, I'll scratch your eyes out, Lumikki thought, but settled for answering with a kittenish meow. Then she outflanked him by handing him her plate to hold and saying she was going to powder her nose. He stood there looking satisfied, obviously imagining that he now had collateral in his possession that Lumikki couldn't get along without. *Jackass*.

In the basement, Lumikki looked around. Directly ahead was a large kitchen where, judging from the sounds, cooks were working at full tilt preparing new, fresh dishes. She heard the sizzling of frying pans, knives chopping against cutting boards and orders being shouted over the din. A steady stream of waiters and waitresses marched through swinging doors carrying trays, bowls and larger dishes. Lumikki watched the flow of food from a dim corner of the room, safely out of sight.

She had caught a few glimpses of Elisa's father, but he always disappeared when she tried to follow him.

Now, as if on cue, she suddenly heard Terho Väisänen's voice from a nearby hallway. He was speaking English with someone. The other person's voice sounded familiar too, but Lumikki couldn't remember from where.

The voices approached. Then Lumikki realised. She had heard the other man's voice when she was being chased in the woods. The Russian.

Lumikki thought for a second. Should she just stay put and pretend she was lost or curious and that was why she was in the basement? Neither of the men would recognise her. She would attract attention though. She was in the wrong place, and too visible, which wasn't a good thing given what she was up to. She really didn't want any of these people recognising her later on the street.

Lumikki tested the nearest door. It opened. Carefully she peeked inside, but no one was in the room. All she saw were several large chest freezers and stacked plastic crates of alcoholic beverages. Some sort of extra storage room, probably. Slipping inside, she waited for Väisänen and the Russian to pass the door.

They didn't. Instead, they stopped.

'I've got something to show you,' Lumikki heard the Russian say in English.

She glanced around. No back door. No place to hide. Nowhere she could go and no way to get out.

No place but the freezers.

Lifting the lid of the closest chest, she peered inside, felt her breath catch and quickly closed it.

Vomit rose in her throat. Her arms and legs trembled. No time to stand there thinking about what she had just seen though. The party was overflowing with gruesome props, but the contents of that freezer were real. Lumikki glanced into the next freezer and sighed with relief. Nothing but a couple of bags of frozen peas at the bottom. Quickly she switched off the freezer. It wouldn't help much, but at least she wouldn't lose all of her body heat instantly as the freezer strained to cool fifty-five kilos of meat suddenly dropped in it from 36.3 degrees Celsius to minus eighteen.

Lumikki saw the door move.

Climbing into the freezer chest, she crouched in the most comfortable position she could manage and then closed the lid just as the men stepped into the room.

The cold began nipping at her bare skin instantly. Apparently she couldn't get away from the freezing temperatures, even indoors. This winter was cursed.

* * *

Terho Väisänen was impatient. He couldn't stand playing Boris Sokolov's games right now. What he wanted was to have time to polish his strategy for convincing Polar Bear that he deserved some proper severance pay. All the rumours said that no one could blackmail or threaten Polar Bear. No one had ever succeeded, though many had tried.

So he would have to negotiate.

'Where is Natalia?' Terho asked, still speaking English.

Boris Sokolov bared his teeth. The expression was probably meant as a smile.

'That's just what I wanted to show you,' Sokolov replied. 'Your Snow Queen is here.'

Väisänen watched in astonishment as Sokolov opened the lid of the nearest freezer.

Lumikki heard the retching sound Elisa's dad made and knew what he had just seen. The image would probably be etched into her retinas for the rest of time. Material for future nightmares.

A young woman in a freezer, naked and dead.

Eyes open, face powder-blue, with dark, dried blood on her lips. A large hole in her stomach.

'What . . . What have you done to her?' Lumikki heard Elisa's father ask, his voice quavering.

'I'd have thought a cop would have seen a dead body before.'

'But, why?'

'Are you really trying to tell me you didn't know? Natalia tried to run off with the money. Your money. Our money. We stopped her. You must have guessed when you got that bag full of blood-stained money.'

'What money do you keep talking about?'

'Your compensation.'

'Damn it, I keep telling you the money never came.'

'That's your problem, not ours. We made the delivery on February twenty-eighth as agreed. Three times a year, on the days you requested. But this time we brought it to your house instead of hiding it in the woods. We thought you'd appreciate such good service.'

'This is . . . nauseating.'

'This is reality. We couldn't afford to let Natalia leave with the money. Losing €30,000 might not hurt, but the possibility of her informing on us would have.'

'I don't . . . I . . .' Elisa's father groped for the words. 'I don't want to have anything to do with you or your men any more. Ever. Is that clear? This wasn't supposed to happen. No one was supposed to die.'

'Oh, but people have. First Natalia and then Viivo.'

'Viivo Tamm?'

'Polar Bear's men. It was no big deal. Sometimes these things just happen. You should try to be professional about it too. There are always losses. Shipments disappear, money gets stolen, people die. It's all part of the business.'

'Try to be professional? Professional? Damn you. You killed a woman!'

Lumikki heard Terho Väisänen's voice break. He was on the verge of hysteria. She could feel her fingers going numb. Her toes already had. Fortunately she had plenty of oxygen in the freezer. So far.

'I offloaded an unreliable employee. And let me give you a

little tip, Terho Väisänen: think twice before you start bitching to me. All I have to do is say the word and you'll be in there next to your whore. Hell, maybe I'll do it myself.'

Väisänen laughed, but there was an edge of desperation to it. 'But you need me. You've needed me for ten years now.'

'Our arrangement has worked impeccably. You've provided us with information and we've revealed appropriate things to you in return. Our drug business has blossomed and your narcotics squad's statistics have never looked better. It's a win-win. I'm the one you have to thank for your promotion. But you listen to me, Terho Väisänen. I don't need you. You're a fly, a speck, to me. I can find a new informant any time I want.'

'That's good to hear, because I'm done.'

'I decide when you're done.'

'No, Boris, it isn't going down like this. What's going to happen is that I'm going to quit and you can't do anything about it.'

Lumikki listened to the silence between the men grow uncomfortable.

'Hmm,' Sokolov finally said. 'If you really did quit, how could I be sure you wouldn't squeal?'

'You'd just have to trust me.'

'No. I'll tell you. I could trust you because if you ever broke your word, you'd find that beautiful daughter of yours at home in your own freezer, just like Natalia.'

'You bastard.'

Lumikki heard scuffling as Elisa's father apparently attacked Sokolov. A moment later came a groan and then silence.

'I wasn't exaggerating when I said I would do you myself if I needed to.' Sokolov sounded out of breath.

'Okay. Okay. I get it. Now put that thing away. I'm sorry I lost my cool.'

'Remember. Your daughter in a freezer. Cherish that image in your mind if you ever start feeling like you might do something stupid. I'll make it come true so fast your head will spin. And you know I'm a man of my word.'

Then Lumikki heard the door open and the men exit.

Not a moment too soon. The cold had started to make her seriously numb, and the places where her skin touched the freezer walls felt like they were getting frostbitten. Lumikki raised her arm to open the top of the chest.

Then the door opened again. Two sets of footsteps. An intense conversation in Finnish.

'I don't get how we can go through this much booze so fast. They're soaking it up like sponges.'

'Better get used to it. This is just the beginning. You should see what it's like after midnight.'

Waiters, Lumikki quickly deduced.

'What do we need most right now?'

'Bubbly. They always drink that at the beginning. Then they start asking for white and red at about the same rate. Maybe a little more red in the winter. After midnight it's mostly harder stuff, whisky and all that. A surprising amount of rum too. And vodka, of course. Some stick with the same thing the whole time, but most of them want variety.'

Take the champagne and get out of here already, Lumikki ordered in her mind. *Go have your gab session somewhere else.*

'Nice. Someone stacked the reds on top of the champagne again, even though I clearly said bubbly on top, red on the bottom. Like I just said, they don't start drinking red wine until later.'

'Big deal. Come on, let it go. Let's just move them out of the way.'

'It is a big deal to me. This whole thing'll blow up in our faces if people can't follow simple instructions. Listen, you have no idea what kind of chaos you're going to see here by the time this is over. It's pandemonium. We'll be carrying drinks with both arms and it'll still run out. Good luck finding some vintage cognac down here after some bonehead messes the system up.'

'Okay, I get it. Let's do this thing.'

Lumikki silently thanked the second waiter for moving things along when she heard them start moving crates. Bottles made muffled clinks.

'Not on the floor. They'll just be in the way there too. Let's put them on this freezer.'

'Isn't there anything important in there? I mean something we might need soon. It would suck to have to keep lugging these crates all over the room. They weigh a ton.'

'There's nothing in there but a few old bags of frozen vegetables. I just checked an hour ago.'

'Maybe I should make sure.'

Lumikki heard one of the waiters grab the freezer lid handle.

Don't open it. Don't, don't, don't.

Then something heavy thudded down on top of the freezer.

'Hey, are you nuts? You could have crushed my fingers.'

'Yeah, but I didn't. Are you going to help, or do I have to do everything myself?'

'Calm down.'

Another thump on the lid. And a third. And a fourth. Four full crates of bottles of red wine.

'Now hop to it and grab that champagne already.'

Clinking of bottles as each waiter lifted a crate. Footsteps receding towards the door.

'Hey, wait a sec,' one of them said, turning back. Steps approached the freezer again. There was a click and the freezer compressor whirred into life.

'Someone must have turned it off by accident. You have to keep these things cold even if there are just a couple of bags of peas in it. You never know when someone might want to dump half a moose in one.'

Steps towards the door again. The door opened and closed. Lumikki was alone in the storage room.

That is if you didn't count the body of the woman named Natalia resting in the adjacent freezer.

Soon there might be two frozen corpses.

24

'Come on! At least try. You have to shoot it in the head before it sees you. We keep losing points.'

'Bite me! I'm doing my best. Stop bugging me. I can't concentrate.'

'Now! Now! Shoot! Damn it, shoot!'

'Oh yeah! His ass is grass.'

'Nice! That's what I'm talkin' about.'

Elisa felt the headache pounding in her temples and the back of her head. She was sitting in front of her laptop staring at a red dot that hadn't moved in hours. That was probably good. It meant that Lumikki had got inside the party. If she were stuck in the trunk of the car, she would have called or sent a text by now. Elisa wasn't willing to think about any of the other alternatives, like the driver or someone else finding Lumikki and making the trunk of the car her temporary resting place.

Fingertips gravitated towards her mouth and Elisa tore at her cuticles with her teeth. Her pink-and-black patterned gel nails had long since been ruined. What did it matter? Things like fingernails and hair couldn't have interested her less right now.

'I think this room could use some new paint. How about red? Make my day!'

That was it. Elisa had had enough. Marching over to the socket, she pulled the Playstation's plug out of the wall. Tuukka and Kasper's roars of protest fell on deaf ears.

Go home and play if that's all you can do. Children.

'Come on, we were totally going to break the record,' Kasper complained. 'We were totally owning them.'

'Can you two even imagine concentrating on this right now?' Elisa asked, pointing at her laptop.

'Come on, baby. That picture hasn't changed for two hours. And it isn't going to change if everything goes like it should. We can't do anything to help Lumikki right now. Or do you think that if all three of us stare at the screen hard enough we can send her positive energy waves or some daft bollocks like that?'

Tuukka had walked up behind Elisa as he talked and now placed his hands on her shoulders. Elisa angrily shook them off. She couldn't stand Tuukka touching her now. Everything about him revolted her. She couldn't believe she had been in love with him once, that just a few days ago she had thought they might end up together again, once they had both had time to prove their own attractiveness with enough other people. That they were going to be the love story of the century.

If there had been no Tuukka, Elisa wouldn't have to be staring at this red dot that represented Lumikki. She wouldn't have to be afraid for Lumikki or for her father. Tuukka had wanted to keep the money. Tuukka had come up with the bright idea of washing it at the school. Okay, Elisa knew she was being unreasonable and that she couldn't really blame everything on this one boy being an ass, but directing her disgust at Tuukka was easier than finding fault with her father.

Father. Daddy, as Elisa still thought of him. She had always been a daddy's girl, especially since her mum had been travelling for work as long as she could remember. This was the daddy she invented silly games with. The daddy she dragged mattresses and blankets and pillows into the living room with to build giant fortresses. Sometimes they even slept in them. This was the daddy who made her pancakes shaped like teddy bears and sang bubblegum pop songs with her at the top of his lungs. The daddy who never got tired of her constant chatter or frustrated with her odd whims. The daddy she cried to about her first broken heart. And barely a year had passed since their last *Star Wars* movie marathon, which always ended in an intergalactic popcorn war. Mum just rolled her eyes.

The past few days had taken from Elisa the daddy she always thought she knew. In place of him she now had this strange man who cheated on Mum with younger women and was mixed up in something dangerous and illegal. Elisa wished she could look her father straight in the eyes and ask him, 'Terho Väisänen, who are you really?'

She was afraid for Lumikki but also afraid of what she might find out. The safest, most dependable part of Elisa's life had been torn away from her, and she wasn't sure whether she could bear hearing any more revelations. Not that she had a choice.

Tapping on his smartphone, Kasper suddenly looked up.

'Uh oh. I just realised something.'

Elisa's pulse sped up. 'Well, what?'

'I doubt they let anyone keep their phones there. Polar Bear is supposed to be super strict about stuff like that,' Kasper said.

'And you just thought of that!' Tuukka snapped. 'How is she supposed to report on the situation then?'

Elisa kept her cool. 'I don't see why that would be a problem for Lumikki. She'll come up with some way to let us know she's all right.'

'You seem to trust her an awful lot,' Tuukka said, looking at Elisa searchingly.

More than I trust you two, Elisa thought. Of course she was grateful she didn't have to spend all night alone in her big house watching the red dot blinking on the screen. But she had decided that once this was all over, she was unilaterally going to put an end to her friendship with Tuukka and Kasper. They were never again going to be the happy trio they used to be.

Elisa's eyes strayed back to the red dot showing the position of the Garmin locator unit. It was supposed to have helped her parents feel reassured when she went jogging alone, but now Elisa only felt dread and guilt knowing where Lumikki was. What was she doing right now? What was she thinking? Elisa started twirling a blonde lock of hair and then put the end in her mouth. Sucking on her hair had soothed her since she was a child. She knew it irritated Tuukka, but she didn't care.

'And if she doesn't tell us she's okay . . .' Kasper left the sentence dangling unfinished in the air.

'Then we follow our original plan,' Elisa said, trying to steady her voice.

'Where was the GPS?' Tuukka asked.

'On her thigh,' Elisa said. 'On a garter strap.'

'And what if someone notices it?' Kasper asked. 'How do we know someone didn't rip it off and throw it in the rubbish and now Lumikki is dead and stuffed in some closet or dumped in the woods?'

Elisa stood up, her fists clenching. It was all she could do not to hit Kasper.

'You stop that right now. Talking like that isn't going to help anything. Both of you shut up until you have something useful to say. Lumikki is there at the party and she's fine and everything is going the way it's supposed to. If she could hear us right now being all panicky she'd probably just laugh in our faces.'

And with that, Elisa marched into the kitchen. She wanted something to calm her nerves. Her eyes landed on her mother's wine rack. Mum would probably never notice one missing bottle. A couple of glasses of red wine would make her thoughts and fears a little softer and easier to bear.

Elisa's fingers were already wistfully stroking the neck of a bottle, but then she decided against it.

No, she had to keep herself sharp. She had to be ready in case Lumikki needed help.

25

Each crate contained sixteen bottles of red wine. There were four crates. Each glass bottle contained 0.75 litres. Lumikki remembered reading somewhere that an empty glass wine bottle weighed 450 grams. Adding in the crates themselves, nearly seventy-seven kilograms of weight was sitting on the lid of the chest freezer. Not a pleasant thought.

Once at the gym Lumikki had managed to leg press 100 kilograms. This wasn't a leg press machine though. This was a freezer.

Lumikki kicked off her high heels. Then, bracing her lower back as well as she could against the bottom of the freezer, she thrust the soles of her feet against the underside of the lid. She pushed. Nothing.

Hypothermia: when a person's body temperature drops below thirty-five degrees Celsius.

Symptoms: shivering, cold sensation, lack of coordination, muscle twitching.

As core temperature continues to fall, the feeling of cold disappears, muscle-twitching stops and mental acuity suffers. Respiratory and heart rates slow. When the temperature drops below thirty degrees, the risk of arrhythmia becomes significant.

At that point the body's self-defence mechanisms begin moving warm blood closer to vital organs and cold blood to the extremities. The hands become disabled. Moving becomes difficult. Unnecessary movement of the extremities can cause cold blood to circulate, and when it reaches the heart the resulting chilling of the heart muscle can cause ventricular fibrillation and even death.

Lumikki was no stranger to severe cold. That fall, after the break-up, she had started swimming regularly in the lake at the Winter Swimming Club's sauna. The cooler the water got, the better it felt. Diving into a hole in the ice for the first time once the lake froze over was one of the most amazing experiences of her life. Winter swimming was like a drug. With tiny ice crystals sloughing off her skin as she climbed out of the water, warmth would flood through her body, leaving her giddy from the endorphins singing in her veins. The feeling was amazing. You just wanted more and more and more.

Lumikki was the odd girl out at the sauna. Most of the regular visitors were old. Some of them wore woollen caps in the steam of the 120-degree sauna and all of them wore the official winter swimming slippers. Lumikki hadn't bought a pair yet. The grandmas and grandpas generally called her 'girlie'. That suited her just fine. Lumikki had never seen anyone else under twenty at the sauna. Occasionally groups of thirtysomething men or women came for raucous stag parties and the like.

Usually the swimming hole – kept open year round by water left running constantly from a hose – was quiet though. Serious swimmers lowered themselves into the frigid water without any squeals or groans. They took a few strokes and then climbed out, standing on the porch of the sauna building for a while, letting their skin steam. Lumikki loved that moment. Seldom in her life had she experienced anything that could be called holy, but when she had visited the sauna one evening a week before Christmas, with lanterns burning on the patio and stars shining in the sky and every cell in her body feeling completely awake after her swim, a strange gratitude overwhelmed her – a mixture of longing, melancholy and joy that contained a germ of holiness. That moment was her Christmas mass, gazing at the stars and the spruce trees laden with snow, standing solemn and immovable.

But while the occasional dip in an icy lake was good for your health, lying in a freezer was not, under any circumstances. Zero-degree water was different to a minus-eighteen-degree coffin.

Right now Lumikki wished she hadn't listened quite so carefully in health class. She banned her brain from thinking about everything lack of oxygen would do to her. She just had to focus on pushing the lid open. It was all the same, whether she moved her extremities too much or used up the oxygen in the freezer too quickly. She was either going to get herself out or she was going to die.

Her legs were like two frozen tree trunks.

Sucking in a deep breath, Lumikki tensed every muscle in her body and pushed, pushed, pushed.

The lid budged a little. Too little. Lumikki's strength ran out, and the lid shut tight again.

Tears welled up uncontrollably in her eyes even though the last thing she wanted to do right now was cry. She just felt so hopeless. Having everything end here was just so stupid and pointless. She didn't want to die. Just as her life had started feeling worth living again after her years in Tampere.

Snow White in a glass coffin. Sleeping her eternal sleep.

No, this story wasn't going to go that way.

Lumikki thought of the girl she had been. The girl she was now. She had never given up. Not even in the darkest moments.

She adjusted her position a bit. Squeezing her eyes tight shut, she concentrated all her strength in her leg muscles. Not for nothing had she done all of those squats and lunges and leg presses and uphill sprints.

Muscles burning? Let them burn. Pain is just weakness leaving the body. And now for one more round. Sing along with the music if it helps!

Lumikki pushed and pushed and pushed. Her quadriceps shook. Pain burned in her thighs. Strange patterns flashed behind her shut eyelids.

She felt the lid lift. She didn't give up, showing her muscles no mercy. She heard the crates shifting. She heard them tip off and fall to the floor. She heard the glass breaking.

A ripple of tinkling glass like fairies ringing enchanted bells. The sweetest sound in the world.

Now she could stand up and push the lid open completely. She was trembling with cold and exhaustion. Red wine and glass shards covered the floor. Pulling her high heels back onto her feet, Lumikki climbed out of the freezer. High heels did have the advantage that only a very small portion of the sole touched the floor. Carefully placing her feet between the shards of glass, she cautiously moved towards the door.

Only now did she realise that she could also have called for help. Maybe someone would have heard.

But that had never even crossed her mind. She had never called for help.

Boris Sokolov looked on as the other revellers began to relax more and more. Slowly he sipped his Jack Daniel's, his favourite whiskey. Polar Bear had remembered. Sokolov wasn't working now, so he could concentrate on drinking and the view. Beautiful women – he was always happy to look at them. In his watching was a touch of melancholy though, since he realised all too well that he was old enough to be these women's father. One of them might be able to keep him company for a night but no longer than that. Sokolov's chance for a normal, long-term relationship had long since passed. Dozens of lonely years with Jack as his only dependable friend loomed ahead of him.

Polar Bear wanted to keep anything illegal out of these parties. A perfectly reasonable precaution. If the police did happen to raid one of them eventually, no one would get nailed for anything. This river of liquor was perfectly legit.

Sometimes Sokolov hated drugs. Yes, they provided him with a job and a comfortable life. A nice house without any neighbours too close. Influence. Women. And no, he wasn't too righteous to refuse a couple of lines of the pure stuff given the right opportunity. But he had never had any interest in shooting up.

His life was full of constant stress though. He had to make sure shipments arrived in Finland. He had to handle distribution, keep dealers in line, find new clients and worry about old clients running at the mouth. He always had too many irons in the fire. Balls were always falling on the floor.

Before, it was enough just to keep all the other Sergeis and Jorges and Mahmuds and Petters off his turf, but now they were fighting the .coms, and @hotmails too. Designer drugs had caught up with normal ones and in some places galloped past. To get those, you simply sat down at your computer, entered your order and then waited for the mailman to arrive. Fighting them was hopeless.

Polar Bear's idea that their target group were the rich, beautiful and successful was great but impossible to implement in practice. In order to make ends meet, they also had to deal to people who were so bottomed out that they could only pay in cash. Who had already sold their laptops or traded them for junk. Whose bank accounts Social Services watched like a hawk. Who didn't have the option of ordering online.

If the business hadn't been so dangerous, Sokolov wouldn't have needed to kill Natalia. In his own way he had cared about her more than he had ever admitted to himself. He had even looked the other way on Natalia and Terho Väisänen's meetings, even though it had been a risk.

Boris had justified it, telling himself that a relationship with Natalia was one more weapon in the arsenal of blackmail he might have to unleash on Väisänen at some point in the future. The stupid cop who swore he was done. He'd see about that. Boris was sure that Väisänen would come crawling back and beg to be let back in. And Boris would agree, of course, but with certain conditions. They had been letting their pet narcotics detective live a little too high on the hog. Väisänen had looked surprisingly sincere when he claimed not to have received the money. Maybe he was even telling the truth. Maybe someone had stolen the plastic bag from the garden during the night. Boris didn't care though. The money was meant for Väisänen, so Boris wasn't going to cry himself to sleep over it. The more important thing was that Väisänen seemed to be over it too. In the future, he wouldn't be getting nearly such large payoffs.

If Natalia had just stayed in line. She'd had a good, secure future ahead of her. The possibility of rising to be Boris's right hand. But she had got restless and started to daydream. Boris had seen it in her, sensing it in her face and tone of voice. He had only needed one visit to Moscow and Natalia's brother had confessed his sister's entire plan.

Boris could have stopped Natalia simply by not leaving the money at his house. But he had wanted to test her, to measure her loyalty. The gauge had swung to the minus side, even though he held out hope until the very end that she would come to her senses. Natalia hadn't left him any alternative but elimination. It was a shame. Boris had so hoped that of all the people in the world, Natalia wouldn't have disappointed him.

The Jack Daniel's slid down his throat, smooth and warm. Still, Boris had to swallow a couple of extra times.

He would get rid of the body the next day.

Today was no time for dirty work.

26

It was approaching midnight. The party had turned louder and more restless. Music thundered. The drinks had switched from sparkling wine to spirits. Women's make-up was beginning to smudge. Men were loosening their ties.

However, it wasn't quite time to cut loose completely, to throw out all sense of propriety and just drink as much free booze as possible, start picking fights and disappear upstairs to 'rest'. The climax of the evening was yet to come.

The arrival of Polar Bear.

That was why Lumikki had stayed too. After escaping from the freezer she had slipped into the ladies' room, removed her evening gown and, standing over the toilet, drenched her arms and legs with warm water from the handheld bidet sprayer. Gradually the feeling returned to her hands and feet. Then she dried herself off with hand towels, pulled her dress back on and fixed her make-up, which had remained in remarkably good shape. Maybe Elisa really should consider cosmetology as a career. At least she had succeeded in conjuring war paint for Lumikki that not only withstood eating and drinking but also freezing.

To the angry women queuing outside the bathroom door she simply raised her eyebrows without saying a word.

Lumikki could have left. She had accomplished her mission. She knew that Elisa's father was working with a drug dealer named Boris Sokolov. That he had been giving Sokolov information and hiding information from the police in exchange for money. Lumikki knew that the body of a woman named Natalia lay in a freezer in the basement and that Boris Sokolov had killed her. The information she had would most likely be enough to land Sokolov in jail. And Elisa's father, of course, but that couldn't be helped.

But still, Lumikki stayed. Her curiosity would never be satisfied until she saw this mythical, legendary figure everyone spoke of in whispered tones. So she continued her tour of the fantasy rooms, which seemed to go on and on endlessly.

One room was completely pink. It probably would have been Elisa's favourite. Or maybe not, Lumikki realised after a few seconds. She felt a slight nausea when she noticed that in among all the marshmallows, unicorns, rosebuds and frilly pillows were hiding various pink sex toys ranging from delicate whips to enormous dildos. Adult fairy tales for every taste indeed. Lumikki continued walking when an intertwined couple staggered into the room looking as if they might start using the goodies the room had to offer at any moment.

The closer the stroke of midnight approached, the more electric the atmosphere became. Everyone was waiting. Everyone was hungry. With ten seconds left, the countdown began. Everyone had gathered in the large ballroom on the second floor. People jostled and shoved.

Ten.

Glancing around, Lumikki saw Terho Väisänen nervously fidgeting with an empty glass.

Nine.

The music was turned down and then went silent.

Eight.

The lights dimmed. Only the stars projected on the ceiling remained.

Seven. Six. Five. Four. Three.

Suddenly Lumikki almost burst out laughing thinking of the absurdity of the situation. Here she was, a regular teenage girl who just happened to walk into the school darkroom at the wrong moment.

Two.

People weren't yelling the numbers out any more. They said them calmly, respectfully.

One.

Darkness swept over the room. Everyone fell silent. A muffled jingling like the sound of distant sleigh bells became audible. From the ceiling flakes began to fall that looked like real snow. When Lumikki touched one of them, it disintegrated.

Suddenly powerful spotlights illuminated the centre of the room.

Two women. Both in Snow Queen costumes. That name fitted them a thousand times better than the frozen Natalia. Identical twins. They had appeared in the middle of the room, as if from thin air. Lumikki couldn't quite guess their age. They could just as easily have been twenty as fifty. From this distance, she couldn't make out any telling wrinkles on their hands or necks.

The ballroom erupted in ringing applause. The women waved majestically. Then Lumikki noticed that one of them was wearing a silver pendant in the shape of an ice crystal around her neck. The other woman's pendant bore a silver bear.

Ice and a bear. Ice bear. Polar Bear. Not one person, two. Who were still just one, singular.

The women waited for the crowd to calm down. Then they began to speak, constantly switching turns so fluidly that Lumikki couldn't quite follow which one was speaking at any given moment.

'Winter is a time of enchantment. That was why I wanted the theme of this celebration to be fairy tales. Dreams, fantasies and nightmares. These are the ingredients of fairy tales. You are all here because I wish to thank you. You have participated in creating a dream. A dream of a society more elegant, more efficient, more purposeful. For us, limits are made to be exceeded, rules to be broken, norms to be challenged. Celebrate! For one moment forget the narrow-minded boxes and expectations of the world outside. This is all for you. Life is for you.'

There was nothing to grab hold of in what the women said. They weren't saying anything concrete. They spoke English without any accent. Even if Lumikki had been carrying a recorder, she wouldn't have got anything incriminating. What were these women involved with? Were they pulling the strings of all of these party guests? How much of their activities were criminal?

Looking over the adoring crowd, Lumikki understood that she would probably never know. Polar Bear's real activities were like the fake snow falling from the ceiling. If you tried to catch them, they disintegrated and disappeared.

She would never have a chance against these people. And the women might simply be a façade. No one would catch them. No one could do anything to them.

Lumikki could put Boris Sokolov behind bars though. The events that began with the blood-soaked cash in the darkroom could come full circle. That would be enough.

Now she wanted to go home.

27

'I don't need a looking glass to tell me you're the fairest woman at this party.'

Hot breath wafted against Lumikki's ear and firm hands grasped her waist. Lumikki swore to herself. Her tormenter had found her again and succeeded in capturing her in a surprisingly tight grip just as she was intending to leave. She could smell from his breath that he had imbibed more than a few shots of cognac. Lumikki could feel from the heavy-handedness of his grip that she had no hope of wriggling free. It would only attract unwanted attention if she tried.

'I was starting to worry that you'd disappeared. That would be unacceptable. We were interrupted so regrettably,' the man whispered, pressing his broad carcass against Lumikki's back.

At least ninety kilos, Lumikki guessed. Might be surprisingly strong when provoked. Time for a different tactic now.

'You haven't gone cold on me already, have you?'

Fortunately not, Lumikki thought.

Turning around, Lumikki looked the man in the face. His eyes were bloodshot. He had left his tuxedo coat somewhere. Large dark-blue patches ran outwards from his armpits across his powder-blue shirt. His tie was a little loose. With a gesture full of false self-assurance, she took hold of the man's tie, drew her mouth to his ear and whispered, 'Let's go upstairs and see if this story has a happily ever after.'

Then she took a nibble of the man's earlobe, forcing down the nausea. She could play this role too.

A satisfied blush spread across the man's face and he licked his lips.

'What are we waiting for?' he asked.

As she climbed the stairs, Lumikki could feel the man's constant gaze on her back. Trying to escape would be pointless. Her legs were trembling a bit, but she forced herself to swing her hips invitingly as she walked. What would it be like to ascend these stairs ahead of someone she really wanted to be with, to pull a door shut behind them and lock the rest of the world outside? The smell of sunscreen and warm skin. Running up the wooden steps of the boat dock at the cabin, laughing. Footsteps following resolutely. Tingling in anticipation as she listened to them come.

Reminiscing was pointless. That had been last summer. An eternity ago.

Now was now, and she should do this.

Lumikki led the man to a free room, in the middle of which was a large wrought-iron bed. She shoved the man down on the mattress. It was important to be as self-assured and bold as possible.

'I knew you were a wildcat! But that's okay. I'll tame you. But kitty can have her fun first,' the man said, beginning to pull his trousers off while still lying on the bed. Lumikki shut the door and turned the key in the lock with a click. Then she sashayed towards the man, who tried to grope her with his sweaty hands.

'Tisk, tisk, kitty wants to toy with you first, remember,' Lumikki said, pushing the man down.

To Lumikki's relief, his drunken eyes lit up. He was at her mercy, at least for the moment. Lumikki climbed onto the bed and straddled her victim, who immediately began stroking her thighs hungrily.

'What's this . . .?' the man asked, his forehead wrinkling in confusion as he found the GPS tracker.

Oh shit. Quickly Lumikki grabbed the man's hands and forcefully pulled them up towards the headboard.

'Now be a good boy,' she whispered, holding the man's wrists with her left hand while she dug something fluffy and pink out of her handbag with her right.

'Oh, so you're into bondage?' the man said with a grin. Lumikki snapped the handcuffs shut around his wrists and then fastened them to the iron bed frame.

'Not really,' she replied and stood up. 'But I hope you are.'

The man took a few seconds to realise that Lumikki had no intention of returning to the bed. When it finally dawned on his cognac-clouded brain and an enraged roar erupted from his lips, it was already too late. Lumikki locked the door from the outside.

Then she walked to the window at the end of the hall. Opening it, she tossed the room key and the key to the handcuffs out into the snow, where they disappeared instantly. That was one less obstacle to her getting home.

Terho Väisänen stared out of a large window into the darkness.

He had given up, realising that there was no way he was going to be able to convince Polar Bear that she should pay him off and let him go. Or they. How was he supposed to address them? He had tried to talk to one of the women's bodyguards and request a meeting. His request was denied. When he explained that he had received a special invitation to meet Polar Bear, the bodyguard coldly informed him that his invitation meant nothing. He shouldn't waste his time imagining that Polar Bear would be interested in a nobody like him.

And when he looked around at the other guests, he understood that the bodyguard was right. He was little more than a gnat to Polar Bear. Even Boris Sokolov was only a gnat or at most a fly. They were ludicrously small players in the larger game.

All Terho could do was leave with his tail between his legs. Go home, hug his daughter and write his wife an email telling her that he missed her. Think about how to make ends meet without his most important source of income. The situation wasn't hopeless. Yes, he had his debts, but he also had a job. And so did his wife. They could cut back on their daily expenditures. He would have to stop gambling of course, but that had been part of his plans for a while now. He wouldn't need money to help Natalia any more, since there was no Natalia. Terho's hands began to shake and he felt sick to his stomach just thinking about that. He had to try not to. He couldn't let that pain take over now. He had to stay rational. He had to think practically. His daughter didn't always need to have the most expensive everything. Slowing down, simplifying their life and spending more time together would do the whole family good. Live a normal life like everybody else.

Normal people's lives didn't include passing information to crime bosses about when and where the police would be conducting their next raid, what dealers were informing, what trucks would be stopped at the border, or what campaigns they were planning to weed out drug trafficking. Normal people's lives also didn't include receiving tip-offs about drug stashes and dirt on small-time crooks Sokolov's gang wanted to get rid of for one reason or another. Over the years Terho had solved an embarrassing number of crimes with Sokolov's help. He had thought that both benefited from their agreement.

Sokolov wanted mastery of the Tampere drug trade, and Terho wanted to lock up the dangerous dealers who sold contaminated mixtures and outright poison in place of genuine product and caused most of the drug deaths.

He had assuaged his conscience by telling himself that Sokolov mostly sold to people who had their habits under control and weren't going to end up in the ER with overdoses. Recreational users. But he had known for a long time that was only part of the truth. Sokolov was perfectly happy to take money from people who would have been better off buying bread and milk for their children. Terho had just wanted to bury his head in the sand.

He wanted to bury his head in the sand now too. Suddenly he was deathly tired. He wanted to leave.

Just then Terho noticed the same young woman whose dress had caught his attention before. Now he also noticed the woman's white beaded handbag. Generally he didn't know the first thing about women's handbags, but that particular one he happened to know a lot about. An Hermés original, it cost hundreds of euros. He knew because he had bought exactly the same bag for Elisa as a birthday present, since she had been begging for it for so long.

A similar evening gown could be a coincidence.

A similar handbag could be a coincidence.

But both of them together on the same woman couldn't be.

With a few steps, Terho strode over to the woman, took her firmly by the arm and demanded an explanation.

Boris Sokolov's interest perked up when he saw Terho Väisänen arguing with some young woman. Moving closer, he grasped enough of Väisänen's Finnish to understand that he was claiming to have bought the woman's handbag and dress. And apparently her shoes.

Boris snorted. Apparently Väisänen had been spending his money on women besides Natalia. That would have to end now too. Boris was already turning back the way he had come when he caught the word *tytär*. *Daughter*.

That stopped Boris in his tracks. His brain raced a million miles an hour. If the girl in the red dress was Terho Väisänen's daughter, it was clear she knew too much. She knew who had chased her in the woods. She might even know about Natalia. And the money. Why else would she be here at the party?

It would be best to go talk to her and make sure she knew to keep her mouth shut just like her father.

Lumikki tried to wrench her arm free of Elisa's father's grasp, but as a police officer he was clearly used to dealing with uncooperative people. His grip was like iron.

'Answer me! Why do you have Elisa's handbag?' Lumikki could see Boris Sokolov approaching. Something about his eyes scared her.

Väisänen was oppressively close.

He sniffed the air. 'You're even wearing her perfume!' he snapped.

Sokolov was only three steps away.

Lumikki had to get away.

Forcefully she shoved Elisa's handbag against her father's chest.

'Fine, take it. Unfortunately I can't return the perfume.'

Väisänen was thrown off-guard enough that his grip loosened ever so slightly. It was enough. Lumikki tore herself away and rushed towards the stairs. She heard Sokolov coming after her, bellowing something in Russian.

At the stairs she ran into a waitress dressed as Alice in Wonderland carrying some sort of dairy-based drinks. Maybe White Russians. Silently apologising, Lumikki knocked the serving tray out of the woman's hands. Liquid and shards of glass spread across the stairs. She heard Sokolov slip and swear.

That bought Lumikki a few extra seconds. Snatching her high heels off her feet, she burst through the crowd, clutching the shoes in her hands. To the front door and out. She continued running along the candlelit path.

Fire walk with me. This whole thing was starting to feel more and more like something from *Twin Peaks*. All that was missing was the dwarf.

Sokolov yelled to the guards on the stairs.

'Stop her!'

The men turned and blocked her way, two refrigerators she wasn't going to get through.

Lumikki suddenly changed direction. Sokolov followed. A high wall surrounded the building on every side. Lumikki ran to the farthest corner. It was dark. The snow stung the soles of her feet, which were covered only by thin tights.

Lumikki quickly felt the wall with her hand. There was nothing to grip. Even a monkey wouldn't have been able to climb it. However, she did find a small hole. Thrusting the point of one of her heels into the hole, she climbed up and stood on the shoe. She nearly lost her balance. Sokolov was almost at the wall.

Shoving the other shoe into the wall heel-first she took another big step up. Sokolov's hand grabbed the hem of her dress.

The hem ripped.

The shoe broke.

The shoe fell into the snow leaving only the heel stuck in the wall. Lumikki's feet flailed in the air without any support. However, her fingers clung to the top of the wall and she just managed to pull herself up as Sokolov's hand grazed her foot.

Lumikki dropped down on the other side, landing in a soft snowdrift. Instead of trying to get over the wall himself, Sokolov took off, running, presumably for the gate. Lumikki started through the snow, which came up to her calves. The hem of her evening gown was ripped on one side, revealing her entire thigh.

Good, Lumikki thought as she ran. Otherwise moving would be harder.

Running in the snow was difficult, and the cold bit with razor teeth. The forest was as dark as blackness itself.

Sokolov was falling further and further behind though. Lumikki sped up. This was the third time in four days that someone had chased her and she had to run away through the snow and cold.

Three tries. In fairy tales, the heroes always got three tries. The first two failed but the third succeeded. Did that mean that she would get away once and for all? Or that her pursuers would finally catch her?

Third time's the charm. Three strikes and you're out. Which one was this?

Suddenly Lumikki felt something painfully scratch her bare thigh. She ignored it. She just ran and waded and struggled on. Finally the sounds of pursuit faded.

Lumikki brushed her thigh with her fingers, which came back covered with something warm and wet. Blood. Sokolov had shot her in the thigh, but luckily the bullet had only grazed her. Blood was flowing copiously though.

Lumikki didn't want to think about it.

She just ran. The forest embraced her like dark water.

But now the poor child was all alone in the great forest. So afraid was she that seeing all the leaves on the trees she knew not whither to turn for help. Then she began to run, and she ran over the sharp rocks and through the thorns, and wild beasts jumped at her but passed by, doing her no harm. On she ran for as long as her legs would carry her and until night began to fall.

28

Once upon a time there was a girl who ran so far her legs wouldn't carry her any more. And then she continued to run, in her mind, in her dreams. Her slender, strong and agile legs dashed over the drifts leaving nary a print in the soft, white snow. She fled as those who know they are free, who know that no one will catch them.

Lumikki teetered on the border between consciousness and oblivion.

She was no longer cold. She was warm. At some level she knew that was a bad thing, but she didn't care any more. She lay on her back in the snow.

She thought of the blood trickling from her thigh into the snow. She imagined how the red would form beautiful spirals in the white, painting a gorgeous pattern that would spread one metre, two metres, across the entire forest.

She saw herself from above as if she were floating ten metres in the air. Black hair against the snow like a halo. An evening gown that, even ripped, glowed as though spun from red rubies. Twisting figures that extended, growing organically.

Beautiful. Not ugly.

* * *

Ugly. Fat. Too skinny. Weird teeth. Irritating voice. Greasy hair.
Dirty shoes. Hairy arms. Stupid. Idiot. Brain dead. Asshole. Whore.

Where did you get those clothes? Out of the rubbish?

Your parents are probably too ashamed to go out in public with you.

If I looked like that, I'd never leave home.

You must be adopted.

No one will ever want to kiss you.

No one could love somebody like you.

Why are you whining? If it hurts, say so. Oh, it hurts? Shut up or I'll give you a real reason to cry.

You're so ugly you actually look better with some bruises.

Words, words, words, words, words, words, words, words. Phrases, sentences, questions, shouts. Pinching, scratching, hitting, dragging, pulling, shoving, kicking.

You aren't those words. You aren't the shouts and names. You aren't the wicked things spat at you like flavourless gum. You aren't the punches or the bruises they cause. You aren't the blood running from your nose. You aren't under their control. You are not theirs.

Inside you is always the part of you that no one can touch. You are you. You are your own and inside you is the universe. You can be whatever you want. You can be anyone.

Don't be afraid. You don't have to be afraid any more.

'I don't have to be afraid any more,' Lumikki whispered quietly to herself.

Steam rose from her mouth.

Still she remembered their faces. Their girlish voices and laughs that echoed, echoed, echoed down the halls of the school even after the day had ended and the building was silent.

She remembered the smells especially well. In the first years, the cloying imitation aromas of scented erasers. Then sweets eaten secretly at recess, hard raspberry candies and liquorice together. A breath in her face, sweet and salty intermixed. Toffee, mango and peppermint lip gloss. Body Shop vanilla perfume, the first one their mothers would let them wear at school. Then later the real perfumes that changed with the day, the mood, the clothes and the trends. Escada's scent of the season.

She learned to recognise them quickly and precisely, smelling them from a distance so she could know when they would turn the corner. Sometimes it helped. Sometimes she had time to get away and hide to avoid seeing them. But usually it didn't help. Then she learned how nauseating perfume really smells when its stench mixes with sweat or how an unwashed urinal in the boys' bathroom stinks when your head is shoved in it and you're ordered to lick the cold, hard porcelain.

She remembered their names. She would always remember them.

Anna-Sofia and Vanessa.

It had lasted from first grade to the middle of ninth. Every year the hands were stronger, the words more cruel, the blows more painful. Lumikki didn't know why the girls had chosen her. Perhaps she had smiled the wrong way or not smiled at all. Perhaps she had the wrong tone of voice at the wrong time. It didn't matter. She had learned quickly that she would never be able to change herself or her behaviour to be good enough for Anna-Sofia and Vanessa so they would leave her in peace.

Lumikki had never told anyone. She had never even considered that an option. Silence had been the general rule at home. Don't ask, don't tell. Everything was good if nothing bad was said out loud. The bruises, the scrapes, the sprained wrists, the ripped clothing. Everything could be explained if an explanation was necessary. School had been a battlefield, and Lumikki could never know who was a friend and who was an enemy. Her strategies had required careful thought. Try to minimise casualties. Telling the teachers would just have made the situation worse. She had to assume they wouldn't believe her. Anna-Sofia and Vanessa knew how to play act in front of the adults. Their smiles were angelic and innocent.

Violence, torture and subjugation. Lumikki had refused to think of what she experienced as 'bullying' because that sounded like something minor, transitory and simple. Just a little fun. Just a little kidding. Just a little shoving. She fell all on her own. It's just an inside joke we have.

In the eighth grade Lumikki had secretly started running and lifting weights. She had decided to be in the best physical condition she could so she could get away. That had worked better every time, but hadn't made the nightmare end.

Then once, on a late, wintry afternoon when the sun had already disappeared below the horizon and the schoolyard was empty, Lumikki hid behind the compost bin until she was sure Vanessa and Anna-Sofia had left. She had endured the stench of banana peels and pea soup leftovers that penetrated the frozen air, radiating with the heat of the decomposition process. She waited until everything was silent. A blue dusk fell over the schoolyard. Peace.

Lumikki left her hiding place. She moved noiselessly. She melted into the grey shadows, little more than a breath of wind on the trampled snow. She heard the sounds of cars blocks away. She heard dogs barking in a distant park. She heard snow sloughing off the school roof. But still she heard Vanessa and Anna-Sofia's footsteps too late. Too late she dashed off on legs filled with explosive power. It just wasn't enough. The girls drove her into the back corner of the yard where high brick walls rose up. Running towards the wall, Lumikki removed her mittens and shoved them in her pockets. After reaching the wall, she grabbed the rough bricks with her fingers and tried to climb. Her feet couldn't find any purchase. Her fingers froze in the cold air and wouldn't hold on. She was trapped.

Lumikki turned, pressing her back against the brick wall and preparing to receive their blows. She had learned how to take a hit. She already knew how best to shield herself. She knew when to breathe in and when to breathe out, when to tense her muscles and when to relax. She just hoped the beating wouldn't last very long today. She was cold and needed to pee. She wanted to go home. She wanted to eat her dad's slightly burned fish sticks and do her homework without thinking anything.

Anna-Sofia and Vanessa approached. They didn't say anything. Silence was worse than insults and threats, condensing into an anticipation that brought the taste of bile to Lumikki's mouth. The girls crept towards her softly, like wolves. But really Lumikki would have preferred to meet hungry, angry wolves than this pair whose hair shone in the dusk, their lips sparkling red. These were much more dangerous creatures, with ice in place of warm blood pumping through their hearts.

Slowly Lumikki counted down from ten, waiting for the first breach of her physical borders. She didn't know whether it would be a light shove on the shoulder, a swift kick in the stomach or a glob of peppermint spit in her face.

Ten, nine, eight, seven . . .

Suddenly Lumikki felt something hot and red growing inside. It was strange. It didn't feel like it was coming from her. Anger. Rage. A blinding desire not to be afraid. The numbers disappeared, thought disappeared, time and place disappeared. Afterwards she could never say what had happened. A piece of her memory was missing. A black hole in the timeline.

She was sitting on Anna-Sofia in the snow, hitting her in the face with all her might. On her knuckles was something warm and dark. Dimly she understood that it was blood from Anna-Sofia's nose. She sensed rather than felt that Vanessa was trying to tear her off. Lumikki's elbow made contact with Vanessa's stomach and the girl let go.

Lumikki didn't know how long she had been pummelling Anna-Sofia. She was watching herself from somewhere far away. A girl with tears and snot running uncontrollably down her cheeks and jaw. Whose arms rose and fell more impotently with every stroke. Was that really her? Wasn't it supposed to be the other way around? Anna-Sofia whimpering and protecting her face, Vanessa holding her stomach and screaming for Lumikki to stop. Wasn't that backwards? Then suddenly Lumikki burst back into her own body, feeling Anna-Sofia's soft, submissive form under her, and then the rage was gone.

She stood up. Her legs trembled. Her hands hung limp. The cold nipped at her fingers. She wiped her wet face. Anna-Sofia sat up hunched over, and Vanessa knelt next to her. They did not look Lumikki in the eye. Lumikki did not look them in the eye.

No one said anything. Silence spoke more clearly than words.

With shaking, exhausted legs, Lumikki set off towards home. She was not afraid that the girls would follow her and try to get revenge. She was not afraid of anything. She did not feel anything. She did not think anything. Halfway home she stopped on the side of the road and vomited. The pea soup looked surprisingly similar to how it had before eating.

At home she slipped straight into the bathroom before her parents could see. The girl who looked back from the mirror was a stranger. On her cheeks were streaks of blood. In wonder, Lumikki raised her hands and touched them. The girl in the mirror did the same. The blood was not hers. It was Anna-Sofia's blood that Lumikki had wiped on her face from her hands. Lumikki washed her face once, twice, three times, four times with water as hot as she could stand. She scrubbed her hands with soap until they stung.

After finally getting into bed that night, she drifted off immediately and slept long into the morning without dreaming. When her phone beeped to wake her up, she felt worse than she ever had before. Worse than when she had been hit and kicked the day before.

Lumikki was sure the incident would not end there. Anna-Sofia and Vanessa would never let it drop. She would be punished one way or another, either officially or not. They would never give up on revenge.

One day passed, then two, three, a week, a month. Nothing happened. Anna-Sofia and Vanessa simply left her alone. Yes, she was still isolated from the rest of her class and no one spoke to her voluntarily, but there was no more hitting. Or name calling. Or text messages threatening to kill her.

Everything just stopped.

Gradually Lumikki began to trust it. She breathed more easily. Spring came, bringing with it more light and fewer school days. As she listened to the others singing '*Den blomstertid nu kommer*', the hymn they always sang at graduation, Lumikki felt something heavy and black release its grip on her. With her ninth-grade diploma in her hand, she walked out into the streaming sunlight, summer and freedom.

The snow shone yellow. Then orange. Then a moment later green. Lumikki saw the lights and heard a pop. Golden stars fell from the sky. Then enormous roses burst into life, their petals opening, melting and vanishing. A unicorn struggled towards the moon. The planets danced. Fireworks.

In honour of Polar Bear.

It was probably almost twelve thirty.

Lumikki thought of the small locator beacon attached to her thigh with a garter strap. She considered the instruction she had given Elisa in case she didn't return from the party or report back by midnight.

She had to leave the party before the clock struck twelve.

But wasn't that a different story? *Cinderella*?

The crackling continued. Lumikki floated on multicoloured waves. She felt good. Just tired.

'*Every evening when the lamp turns out and real night arrives.*'

Wasn't that how the lullaby went?

Wasn't that how the blue dream began?

Blue, blue, sparkling blue.

For a moment Lumikki thought the fireworks were still going. Then she realised that she wasn't hearing explosions any more. A wailing started.

A white wall. A sterile smell. Bright lights.

Sickening, pulsating pain somewhere far away. Lumikki couldn't think about it. The taste of antibiotics in her mouth.

Drip, drip, drip. Something was flowing into her. She was attached to something. Dimly she remembered that there were names for all these things surrounding her. She didn't have the strength to think of them though.

Figures moving in front of the lights.

Familiar faces.

Mum. Dad.

Sounds from far away, behind glass, above the surface of the water, on the other side of a wall.

'The doctor said she's turned a corner. Don't cry, dear. *Älskling*. She'll be all right. She's a fighter.'

'I just can't stop thinking. I couldn't stand it if we lost her too.'

'We won't. Hush. Hush.'

Her too? Who had Mum and Dad lost? Lumikki wanted to ask, but she couldn't form the words. Opening her mouth would have taken an overwhelming effort. She just wanted to sleep. She would have to remember to ask later. Sometime later. After she had slept for a hundred years.

But wasn't that a different story? *Sleeping Beauty*?

Lumikki felt herself sinking into the bed, into its softness, slipping through the mattress as if through layers of cloud, and flying.

EPILOGUE

FOUR MONTHS LATER

On the card was a black-and-white photograph of a muscular naked man holding a kitten in a strategic location. Lumikki didn't even need to turn the card over to guess who it was from.

Hey Girl!

Everything's okay here. Mum isn't as nervous as before and I'm sleeping through the night without waking up all the time and don't look behind myself all the time when I'm walking down the street. It's been good for me to be free for a while. I'm applying for beauty school here. If I get in, I start in the autumn. I'm pretty sure that's going to be my thing.

Jenna

P.S. I'm already used to my new name. I don't turn around any more when someone shouts my old name on the street or something.

P.P.S. I haven't been to see Dad. Maybe some day. I still can't do it. I'm sure you understand. I can't even write anything about it without starting to cry.

P.P.P.S I knitted you some gloves. They'll come in the mail later. Sorry it took a while. You won't need them any more, but you'll have them next autumn.

Lumikki smiled. She glanced out the window. Elisa – well, Jenna now – was right. It was already the end of June, a bewilderingly hot one. Everything was blooming and fragrant and radiant.

It was good to hear she was doing well. Her dad had gone to jail, along with Boris Sokolov. Their cases had been processed with unusual speed. The police had probably wanted to get a blank slate as quickly as possible and start cleaning up their image. Both had received long sentences. Sokolov's Estonian sidekick Linnart Kask had also been sent to prison. Elisa and her mother had moved to another part of the country and changed their names. That was probably smart under the circumstances. Elisa had sworn up and down to Child Protection Services that she was done with drugs. Lumikki believed her. Elisa and her mum would have to find a totally new way to live their lives and be a family. That wasn't necessarily all bad.

Lumikki's left hand gravitated to the short-cropped hair at the back of her neck. She still wasn't used to such a short hairdo, although it did feel liberating. Once the light roots of her dyed black bob had sprouted to the point where she looked as if she was going bald, she had made the decision. A never-ending spiral of hair dying wasn't appealing, and she also wasn't particularly interested in how the combination of fair skin and dark hair drew attention to her name. So, super-short hair and her own natural colour it was. She also liked how simple it was.

In a way, Lumikki felt safer having a completely different girl staring back from the mirror to the one who had attended Polar Bear's party. Not that she was actually afraid of anyone from the party recognising her on the street. People were surprisingly blind when visual images were removed from their original contexts. Because no one could imagine that a girl with no make-up traipsing down the street in old combat boots and a green army jacket could ever have been at a high-class party, the conclusion was obvious: she hadn't been there. The human mind was just that simple. So stupid, but so lucky for her.

Over the past two months, Elisa had sent Lumikki cards a few times before. Lumikki kept them under the false bottom of the top drawer of the dresser in her old room.

Yes, she was living at home again. In Riihimäki, that is, in the house where she grew up. After the events of the winter, the police had interrogated her first and then her parents had. She had told both only the bare necessities. Her parents had demanded that she move back home 'at least for the time being'. Lumikki tolerated it even though her old room was so full of the past and felt so small. She went to school by train, even though that meant waking up at an inhuman hour.

For the time being.

Lumikki thought she would be able to convince her parents over the summer that it was safe for her to live alone again in Tampere.

No one looked at her strangely at school because no one knew. Kasper and Tuukka had been expelled when the drug party and school break-in had come out. Everything had been handled as quietly as possible. There were rumours around school, of course, but no one knew to connect Lumikki to them. Some of the rumours were pretty wild, but none of them even approached the insanity of the truth.

Terho Väisänen was in prison. Boris Sokolov was in prison. Polar Bear was not. Were not.

Lumikki had kept her mouth shut tight about them in her interviews. She knew that if she blabbed, she would only be hurting herself. She didn't have any evidence that the twins were involved in anything illegal. She didn't actually know anything about them.

And the police didn't ask. The party venue had been in Boris Sokolov's name, and everything else had been operated through him too. Officially there was no Polar Bear. No one had seen them, no one had ever heard of them. It didn't matter whether they were a he, a she, an it or a they.

Lumikki idly stroked the edge of the postcard. Strange that Elisa preferred to send cards than to write emails. That was another flaw in her shiny image, an aberration that to her own surprise made Lumikki really like her. She had thought of Elisa when painting a tiny pink rose in the bottom corner of her *Girlfriends* painting. You wouldn't even notice it unless you looked closely.

She put the card with the others. Under the false bottom of the dresser drawer was also an envelope she had received immediately after her release from the hospital. Inside were two €500 notes. One thousand euros. It was such a small part of €30,000 that no one would miss it. She didn't know whether Elisa, Tuukka and Kasper had hidden any more. She didn't want to know.

One thousand euros was enough of a secret.

Lumikki was used to having secrets. She had always had them; sometimes big, sometimes small. Closing the dresser drawer, she imagined she was also putting away the other secrets she didn't have any concrete evidence to prove.

Polar Bear and the fact that she had seen them.

Anna-Sofia and Vanessa and what they had done to her during elementary and middle school.

The important person whom Mum and Dad had lost but whom she hadn't been able to work up the courage to ask about since coming home from the hospital. In a house furnished with taboos, you didn't just start redecorating like it was nothing.

And one more secret. The one whose picture Lumikki was holding now. Of course, a photograph was physical evidence that the person in it was real, but nothing proved that Lumikki had loved him. That he had loved Lumikki. If he had. Lumikki wanted to believe he had.

She stroked the picture carefully with her thumb. Short, light brown hair varying in hue from wheat to hazel. A cheek, a shoulder, an arm. Captivated once again by those eyes so blue they brought a purebred husky to mind. Some people thought those eyes were piercing, scornful. Lumikki saw deeper. She saw the warmth, the uncertainty, the joy, the light.

Longing clenched her stomach with astonishing strength. Lumikki thought it would have eased by now. She was as wrong as wrong can be.

The name was already tingling on her lips. The name she

had whispered and cried aloud. She wasn't over it yet. She wasn't ready to move on like that. Not now, perhaps not ever.

Lumikki locked the drawer, even though she knew that was an unnecessary precaution. She held the small, tarnished key in her hand. It gleamed, but dimly. It was plain and inconspicuous.

Once upon a time there was a little key that could have fitted in any lock.

Fairy tales don't begin that way. That is how other, brighter stories begin.